Every Time I See You Falling

Written by
Elaine Corum Strawn

Paperback ISBN: 978-1-7343673-8-6

Cover design by Alexandria Rogers
Interior design by Liz Schreiter

Join our conversation on social media.

@off.and.running
@offandrunningpublications
@offandrunning_
OffandRunningPublications.com

Contact the author at strawnelaine@gmail.com

Other books written by Elaine Corum Strawn

Strokewaves

Kiddie & the Major

Going on a Bear Hunt

Lessons Learned in a Primary Classroom

Other books from Off & Running

Ornithomancy by Mollie Jackman

Crooked Lines by Dyarl Lewis

Edgewood Village by Linda Koenig

Warren's Hill by Linda Koenig

My Name is Annabella by Beverly Miles

There's a Snake Down There by RGO Books

This book is dedicated to all the book lovers out there, who give authors a chance to make their dreams come true. I'm so happy you found your way here and thank you for your patience while I work on writing your next favorite bestseller. Happy reading!
—*Elaine Corum Strawn*

"The saddest thing about betrayal is that it never comes from your enemies; it comes from those you trust the most."

"Without a rich heart, wealth is an ugly beggar."
—*Ralph Waldo Emerson*

ONE

Chelsea's body throbbed dully, as her mind struggled to know where she was. She was vaguely aware of a bright white light and for just a second, she wondered if she was quite possibly dead. Oddly, she comforted herself with the thought that it didn't seem likely as she was pretty sure she would never be welcomed into the pearly gates of heaven. She became aware of muffled voices as she willed her eyes to open and figure out where the flip she was. She heard a frantic voice yell for more anesthesia just before she felt her mind drift off.

Despite her effort to resist, she found herself drifting back to the sound of a gunshot followed by severe pain ripping through her abdomen. She realized she was falling, but could do nothing to catch herself. She lay on the floor, dismayed to see her life pass before her eyes. It was a short list of people who had loved her and an even shorter list of happy memories. As Chelsea lay there bleeding, she kept thinking to herself how easy it would be to let go, doubting anyone would much care. However, she quickly jerked herself back at the thought of going to hell. She wasn't the most religious person, but she most definitely believed in an afterlife.

Chelsea moaned when suddenly someone was pushing on her abdomen, making the pain unbearable. Slowly she realized someone was talking to her, their soothing voice reassuring her everything was going to be okay, she was going to be okay. Briefly she opened her eyes to see Kat's worried face looking down on her. It took every effort on her part to ask if Thomas was okay. Chelsea was puzzled to see tears rolling down Kat's cheeks as she nodded yes. Thank god Thomas was safe.

Chelsea realized she could faintly hear a man's voice now, also reassuring her, telling her she was strong, that he was on his way, and he would see her soon. Although his voice seemed far away, Chelsea knew in her heart that it was Alex. It was good to hear him encouraging her, relieved that he didn't sound mad anymore. She couldn't blame him for that after asking to borrow a million dollars. It had been a ridiculous request, but the sad truth was she had no one else to turn to.

Chelsea knew she didn't deserve him, but she thanked god for Alex. Maybe she was more religious than she realized. Or maybe she wasn't the horrible person she believed she was after all. She reminded herself she had deliberately sought him out, setting the trap to get him to give her what she wanted.

Damn! She was that horrible person. A job with his publishing company had been her goal, but in the end she had got much more than that. Somehow, Alex and Chelsea had grown a relationship too. She wasn't sure where it was going, but they definitely spent a lot of time together for both professional and personal reasons.

Now as Chelsea lay bleeding profusely on the floor, she chose to focus on Alex. Hearing his voice had been the reality check she needed. Even as the pain was shutting her brain down, it took very little effort for her to walk down memory lane, back to the first time she said hello to Alex.

TWO

The Gotham Hotel stood in Midtown Manhattan, the boutique hotel's sleek and modern design appealing to Chelsea. She checked her watch one more time as she waited for the elevator to reach her floor, knowing she would find the bar at the back of the hotel. The extra steps barely registered with Chelsea's Louboutins as she rehearsed her lines for her latest target, confident that he would be there. If she had learned anything about him, he was, at the very least, predictable with his daily routines.

As she entered The Reading Room, she quickly scanned the bar, searching for a certain tall, dark, and handsome someone. She mentally checked herself before wandering over to the bar, striving to be casual and approachable. Chelsea had dressed down tonight, wearing cream dress pants with a cream silk blouse, her outfit cinched at the waist with a gold Coco Chanel belt. She liked to think of it as her lucky belt, needing all the help she could muster to start her newest adventure off on the right foot. As Chelsea sat her bag down, she quickly commanded the bartender's attention.

"I'll have what he's having." she told the bartender, turning her head in the direction of her target.

The stranger turned towards her, taking his time to size her up before informing her doubtfully, "I'm drinking a whiskey sour."

"Perfect! Make the bourbon Woodford Reserve please, fresh sour, skip the egg white. Thank you." She nodded to the bartender, dismissing him to fetch her drink.

She shimmied onto her barstool, leaving an empty one between her and him, pretending to be busy digging in her bag for something or another.

Convinced she had rummaged long enough, she looked up, pleased to see he was watching her. "Seems like you know your way around a whiskey sour."

Chelsea smiled as she sat her phone on the bar, making a show of checking for messages before turning to answer him. "It's not my first choice of cocktails, but after my day, it will hit the spot."

"And what would be your first choice?" he asked, glancing up briefly as the bartender sat her drink down in front of her.

"Champagne of course!" Chelsea said with a big smile. "You know it's been a good day when you're drinking champagne."

Chelsea picked up her drink, turning to the stranger before raising her glass to him. "Cheers to new chapters!" she said before taking a generous sip.

"Cheers," he said as he raised his glass in return.

She asked the bartender for a menu when he came back around to confirm that her drink was satisfactory. She realized she was starving as her busy day had not left her any time for lunch. She took her time perusing the menu, trying to choose between the grilled asparagus salad or the Reading Room burger with hand cut fries. She loved a good aioli and appreciated that they generously added two to their burger. In the end she asked for the burger, cooked medium rare. She watched as the bartender soon returned to set a burger and fries down in front of her handsome stranger.

"Smells divine." she said almost to herself. He hesitated for only a moment before pushing his plate towards her.

"Would you like a few fries to hold you over until your own arrive?" he asked generously.

Chelsea leaned over to gingerly pick two off his plate. She held his gaze as she blew on them before popping the hot potatoes into her mouth.

"Thank you." she said with a smile. "Delicious."

"So. Tell me about this new chapter. Are you new to New York?" Chelsea hesitated, pretending to be unsure how much she should share with a stranger.

"I am actually, ummm?" she looked at him quizzically, clearly waiting to be properly introduced.

Wiping his hands on his cloth napkin, he held his hand out to her. "My apologies. Alex Butler. Welcome to New York."

Chelsea took his outstretched hand, completely unprepared for what his warm, strong hand did to her. She tried not to sound breathless as she returned the introduction. "I'm Chelsea. Chelsea Botard. Actually it's Chelsea Logan. Soon to be single again."

She took a sip of her drink, unnerved that his expression was hard to read and his handshake causing her to ramble. Changing the topic at hand she asked, "Are you a New Yorker, Alex?"

She waited patiently as he finished his drink, signaling the bartender for another. "Not a native, but I've been here awhile. I moved here permanently after graduating from Columbia University. What brings you to New York?" Alex asked.

"It was time for a new chapter and I decided to give New York a try. I like big cities and that this one is far from home. And ex-husbands." She threw her bait again, hoping he would bite. She didn't have to wait long.

Seeing the bartender headed toward her with her own burger and fries, she unrolled her silverware, before answering his predictable question of "And where's home?"

"I'm from the midwest. Kansas City to be exact." she said before taking her own big bite of her burger. It was heaven.

"Really." he said, more of a statement than a question. "I'm from Chicago. So are you a big Chiefs fan?" Alex asked.

"Yeah no. I don't do sports." Chelsea was quick to shut that down.

"So what's your favorite bar-be-que place? Arthur Bryant's? Jack Stack?" he asked.

Chelsea was surprised to hear him be so specific, but she quickly shut that down too. "I don't do BBQ either."

Chelsea laughed when Alex rolled his eyes at her. "Please tell me you've taken a carriage ride around the Plaza at Christmas? When she stared at him blankly, he gave her one last chance. "How about ice skating? At Crown Center?"

"Yes! When I was in middle school. We skated almost every Saturday. You sound like you've been to KC?" This was news to Chelsea and she listened, completely intrigued by his answer.

Alex shrugged casually. "When the airfare was cheap enough, my family made a few trips during December to enjoy all the holiday hoopla."

"Lucky you." Chelsea said dryly.

Alex laughed before saying, "Yeah, something like that." She was thankful when he switched gears. "So what do you do for fun?"

Just like that her window of opportunity opened. "I read books. I find them to be way better company than most people I know."

Alex nodded in seeming agreement. "A good book is one way to spend your down time. What's your favorite genre?"

Chelsea answered quickly. "I like a good mystery, a good whodunit. But I actually read a variety of books. I'm currently learning to appreciate historical fiction."

She could sense Alex thinking about what she said. She knew he had his own expertise with books and waited to see if she had passed his test. "What are you reading right now?" he asked.

Chelsea smiled to herself, ready with her answer. "I'm reading *Cleopatra* by Stacy Schiff. She was a woman after my own heart. Going after what she wanted and doing what needed to be done. Cleopatra I mean."

"I've never read it." Alex answered. Feeling him pull back from her, Chelsea finished her dinner and drink, deciding it was time to call it a night. She signaled to the bartender.

"Can you put this on my room tab please?" She asked him.

"Good to meet you Alex." Chelsea said, deciding to keep it simple.

Chelsea felt her pulse quicken when he turned on his barstool to face her head on, his handsome face all hers to admire. "Good to meet you too Chelsea. Good luck with your new chapter."

Disappointed with his answer, Chelsea forced herself to maintain her smile as she climbed off her barstool. She found herself falling forward until Alex was catching her, bringing her up close to him. She found herself all but blushing as his touch sent heat through her from head to toe.

"Easy there." He was smiling as he said it, but Chelsea was too distracted by his presence to be witty with her response.

"I'm so sorry! Thank you for catching me." she said, appreciating that his hands were still on her waist.

He seemed to realize it too, suddenly releasing her, but still holding her gaze as he said softly, "Good night Chelsea."

"Good night Alex." Chelsea said back.

Picking up her bag, she gave Alex one last glance as she headed out. He was watching her, his expression still unreadable. Nevertheless, Chelsea had a big smile on her face as she headed for the hotel side of the building. For the most part, she was satisfied with how the night had gone, applauding her last minute performance of falling into his arms.

She was fairly confident he would be there again tomorrow night, just as she would be. As Chelsea got off the elevator and unlocked her door, she was still smiling. It felt good to have something to look forward to for a change. Tomorrow was another day and Chelsea couldn't wait to initiate stage two. After all, what Chelsea wanted, Chelsea usually got. Time would tell.

THREE

Chelsea sat on her bar stool sipping her glass of pinot grigio, trying not to swing her legs in nervous anticipation. She had her menu laying in front of her, deciding to go with the grilled asparagus salad tonight. She had just finished giving the bartender her order when her handsome stranger appeared at her elbow.

"Hello again. Looks like you've had a better day today?" he asked. Chelsea's confusion was short lived as he pointed to her glass of wine. "No bourbon tonight."

"Hello yourself. It *was* a better day, thank you. Much less frustrating and way more productive." She answered warmly.

She waited as he ordered his whiskey sour and then sat down beside her on the barstool next to her. Chelsea's body tingled as his leg grazed hers under the bar. She had her lines ready to go. "So, do you come here often?"

He took his drink from the bartender and then turned to give her his full attention. "You could say that. My office is around the corner."

"Seems like a great area for an office." Chelsea said, picking up her glass of wine to sip, watching him over the rim.

"We do okay. Tell me about your day." he said, steering the conversation away from himself.

Chelsea was happy to get into it, mentally telling herself that it was go time.

"I finalized my lease today for an apartment not that far from here. It's on the Upper East Side and I have a great view of Central Park. The apartment is just what I was looking for. Or it will be when they finish some minor updates for me." Chelsea paused to take another sip of her wine. Alex sat patiently, waiting for her to continue.

"I heard back from some of the resumes I hand delivered yesterday and have some interviews lined up for tomorrow. I'm hoping to have a job by the end of the week." Chelsea threw it out to him and the universe, willing her plan to come true.

"And what kind of employment are you hoping for?" Alex asked, his eyes focused on hers.

His gaze was so intense, Chelsea hesitated for a moment before answering him. "I'm hoping to be a junior editor somewhere. I have a degree in marketing, but I worked for a prestigious publisher in Kansas City. I'm hoping that opens doors for me."

Alex turned his barstool to face Chelsea directly, his words catching her off guard. "So that's what this is about. With all your snug little dresses I thought you were trying to seduce me. But you already know I'm with Hudson & Butler Publishing, don't you?"

He crossed his arms across his chest and sat back on his barstool, daring her to deny it. She managed to squeak out "Excuse me?" sounding as offended as she could.

"I noticed you here before last night. You were sitting at the far side of the bar when I was here for lunch last week. Don't tell me you've already been to my office! I better not be one of your interviews tomorrow!" Alex did not bother to disguise the annoyance he felt.

Chelsea had assumed her sunglasses and oversized hats would have disguised her, but apparently Alex paid attention to his surroundings more than the average man. Part of her wanted to smile at the thought he had noticed her, but the other part was frantically searching how to get herself out of this hot spot.

She took a deep breath and launched in, her words coming out easier than expected. "Okay, okay. You're right. I may have stalked you just a little and yes, it is because I want a job with Hudson & Butler."

He was surprised she was coming clean, expecting her to try to lie her way out of it. "Keep going. Why Hudson & Butler?"

"A few weeks ago there was an article in the Washington Post written by a friend of mine, Katherine Bell. She was writing about the traditional publishing houses versus self-publishing. Do you remember?" she asked. When he nodded, she continued.

"She quoted you a few times so I did some digging and discovered you're one of the most prestigious publishing houses in New York City, which is why I'm sure Katherine came to you as well. I just really need a job and well, I like to work with the best. Apparently that's you."

Chelsea was shocked she was being so honest, realizing the truth was much easier to tell than the lying she was used to. She did neglect to add once she saw his picture in the article, there had been no turning back. He was one handsome executive and seducing him was also part of her plan, but that would come later, after her name was on a contract.

Alex continued to stare at Chelsea trying to decide just how annoyed he was. "Do you have a resume with you?"

Chelsea jumped off her barstool, turning to open her bag and pull one out. As she turned back to him, she could feel his eyes moving over her. She was confident in her leopard ruched skirt, knowing it hugged all her curves, her black sleeveless turtleneck highlighting her tanned arms and blonde curls. She handed her perfumed resume to him as she smiled and said, "Here you are Mr. Butler." She made him move his eyes away first, waiting for him to peruse her resume.

He looked over it briefly before laying it on the bar and asking her. "So, what do you already know about Hudson & Butler?"

Chelsea searched his face briefly before launching in. "I know that you're the Butler and Hudson is a silent partner and the start-up money behind the company. You actually do quite well making you now the money behind the company. I know you've spent the last ten years growing the company and employ roughly a hundred people from the top to the bottom. And I know your office is around the corner and made an educated guess you would come in here sometimes after work. I mean it's called the Reading Room and reading is your thing. Mine too actually." Chelsea stopped abruptly, afraid she had started to ramble.

Alex's expression was noncommittal as he asked another question. "So as a junior editor, what would you bring to the table? Why should we make you part of our team?"

Chelsea's heart stopped for a minute. Was he actually interviewing her right here on the spot? Chelsea repositioned herself back onto her bar stool, stalling for a minute to choose her words carefully. She looked into his eyes and gave him her best shot.

"I'm sure at Hudson & Butler you surround yourself with people such as myself, intelligent and creative. Just like me, they are also hard workers, but I use my intelligence to work smarter not harder. I'm happy to collaborate, but I'm very independent and don't need to be micromanaged. I know when I'm doing a good job and I know when to ask for help. I'm extremely well read and tuned into social media. Not only do I recognize what readers want, I know how to nurture your carefully chosen authors to give us the very best version of their book. Which will eventually make them New York Times Best Sellers, and you, lots of money."

She could see Alex was trying to contain a small smile, his eyes never leaving hers. "So now tell me, what are your weaknesses?"

Chelsea worked hard not to roll her eyes. She knew it was a standard question in an interview and she searched quickly to find the perfect answer. "I suppose some would say that I set my goals high and have a hard time being told no. I'm tenacious with a plan, and I'm not afraid of the work to make it happen. But not everyone always appreciates my plan, despite my hard work. And best intentions." She bit her bottom lip to keep from smiling, trying to maintain her earnest demeanor.

Chelsea could not take her eyes off of Alex, waiting to see what he would say next. "IF I give you a job, I would see this as a personal favor, considering that you've skipped all the traditional formalities of becoming employed with us. "

Chelsea held her breath as she asked, "Meaning what?"

"Meaning I'm happy to help someone starting a new chapter in life, but I am always the boss, *especially* when I tell you no. Does that work for you Ms. Logan?"

Chelsea was all smiles. Leaning forward she said, "That absolutely works for me. And just for future reference, I'm very good at returning favors. I'm here for you, anything you need. When do I start?"

Alex laughed, releasing the tension between them. "You don't let up, do you? Why don't you come in on Monday and make it official. You can sign your contract and I'll show you to your office, but don't expect much for a junior editor."

Chelsea turned and caught the bartenders eye. "Can we get two glasses of champagne please? And put it on Mr. Butler's tab, thank you."

In no time the two were holding their flutes out to each other. "Thank you Alex. You have no idea how much this means to me. Cheers to a new chapter and the beginning of a beautiful partnership!"

Alex extended his flute to hers with a "Cheers!" adding a big smile. He could hear the warning bell at the back of his brain, knowing he should know better. The rest of him ignored it, not the least bit worried this girl could be trouble. He had to admit he looked forward to finding out just how much trouble.

FOUR

Chelsea was showered after her run, her smoothie in one hand as she headed out. She paused briefly outside the doors of the hotel, ready to enjoy a beautiful day. She was headed south of the Gotham Hotel, ready to learn more about the local bookstores. She wasn't sure as a junior editor that she would be responsible for marketing the book once the book was the best version of itself, but Chelsea planned to take more than one book from start to finish, all the way to the New York Times Best Seller List. She smiled thinking about one book in particular she had in mind. For now, Monday would come soon enough, and she decided to enjoy her day of browsing some well known bookstores in Manhattan.

The day passed quickly as Chelsea worked her way through the Rizzoli Bookstore first and then The Strand Book Store. She made a point to introduce herself to whoever ranked highest on the chain of command on a Saturday, pleased and proud to associate herself with Hudson & Butler, leaving her newly acquired business cards. Always confident in her latest plan, she had taken the liberty of ordering them a few weeks ago, well before she had met Alex Butler. After chatting and leaving an impression, Chelsea was happy to browse their books, familiarizing herself with each store's layout of the latest best reads.

Before she knew it she was back at the Gotham Hotel, needing to get ready for her evening. She was pleased to see her dress had been delivered to her room and hung in her closet with a note stuck to the bag, the simple message of "enjoy" attached. She ordered room service, requesting The Reading Room burger and fries. She was beyond famished and more than happy to answer the discreet knock.

She ate most of the burger before trashing the rest, resisting all but a dozen of her fries. Her dress hung on the closet door, reminding her the day's work was not done.

She stood in front of the full length mirror on the door, turning this way and that to check herself in the dress. It was a long dark green satin mermaid dress with a criss cross halter, a long bow making the low back more discreet. What Chelsea loved most about the dress was the way the fabric loosely hugged her curves, making her a knockout in any crowd. There would be important people to meet tonight, an opportunity to start building her contacts here in New York City. As she headed to the elevator she had to admit to herself she mostly wanted the attention of one person in particular.

Chelsea made certain she arrived fashionably late, wanting to make an entrance that was sure to be noticed. She could only hope Alex was somewhere close by and able to witness it for himself.

The fundraiser was in full swing as Chelsea walked in, a room full of well dressed socialites. She was all smiles as she accepted a glass of champagne from a nearby server, grateful for the distraction as she took in the room, searching for where she should head to first. As it turned out, the decision was made for her.

"Well, well, well, look what the cat dragged in." It was Alex, sizing her up as he greeted her. Chelsea was stunned to see how good he cleaned up, the tuxedo he wore making his handsome features even more attractive.

"Why am I not surprised to see you here tonight?" he asked, cocking his head to one side, his eyes locking into hers.

"Oh hello Alex. I wasn't expecting to see anyone I know at the Heart Ball." Chelsea acknowledged, a little annoyed to be compared to something a cat would drag in.

"And yet, here you are anyway." Alex mumbled as he took a sip of his own champagne.

Chelsea could feel herself start to bristle. "Well if you must know, the Heart Ball is a big tradition in Kansas City, so I thought this might be a good way to meet some new people and support a worthy cause, one close to my heart." Chelse smiled to herself, realizing her unintended pun.

Alex had the grace to look properly chastised. "My apologies. You look absolutely stunning. Allow me to help you meet some new people." With a nod and a smile Chelsea accepted the arm he offered her.

As they moved and mingled throughout the room, Chelsea took note that Alex received his own fair amount of attention as he introduced her to a variety of people. She nodded her head when he asked if she would like to get some hors d'oeuvres. It was your typical buffet of cheeses, fancy crackers, pates, meats, and caviar. Chelsea lightly filled her plate, happy to follow Alex to a table where a server magically appeared with more champagne.

"So, how does this Heart Ball compare to yours?" Alex asked.

"It's much the same actually." Chelsea said with a smile. "A room full of people with a lot of money and time on their hands using a worthy cause to make them feel better about themselves."

"Ouch! Seems a little cynical." Alex said, his eyes on her.

"Really? You think all these people are here for personal reasons?" Chelsea said, her hand sweeping the room in general. "Why are you here Alex?" She asked, curious as to what he would say.

Alex studied her for a beat before answering in a solemn voice. "I'm here because my dad had a heart attack and died when I was seventeen. So yeah, tonight is personal."

Chelsea was stunned, mentally kicking herself and unsure what to say next. She finally stammered out, "I'm so sorry Alex. I didn't know."

Alex shrugged, graciously letting her off the hook. "How could you? I'm just saying, people are here for different reasons. When I saw your grand entrance, I immediately assumed you were here because somehow you knew I would be." He left the sentence dangling, clearly waiting for her to deny it.

Chelsea cleared her throat before answering him back. "To be honest, I did see it on your calendar when I dropped my resume off earlier this week. I thought it could be a good opportunity to start building my contacts in New York City. But it is actually an event my family supports every year in Kansas City." Chelsea finished lamely.

By now Alex knew Chelsea had been to his office to play Nancy Drew, looking for ways to literally get her Louis Vuitton shoe in his door at Hudson & Butler. Suddenly the band was playing one of Chelsea's favorite songs. Grabbing Alex's hand she headed to the dance floor, leaving him little choice but to follow her.

"I don't dance!" Alex shouted above the music.

"Just do what I do!" Chelsea shouted back. She was pleased to see Alex watching her as she danced her way through the song "Celebration," although less hip and more swanky with the band's version. Way too soon they had moved their way through the song, the dance floor packed with people not taking themselves too seriously.

Taking advantage of their full dance floor, the band switched gears, moving into a ballad. Chelsea tried to make a retreat back to their table, but Alex quickly grabbed her hand, pulling her into him. Chelsea wondered if her face was red, reflecting the heat she felt being held in his arms. She tried not to listen to the lead singer croon about a man loving a woman. It was all she could do to resist her urge to lay her head on Alex's chest.

"Relax Chelsea." Alex said into her ear, his warm breath making her tingle even more. As the song finished, Chelsea felt herself drawn to look up at Alex, his gaze sending shivers down her from head to toe.

As the group on the dance floor broke into applause, Alex took her hand, leading them back to their table. She felt him give a sudden pause as he realized someone was standing beside their table.

"Aren't you two sweet out there on the dance floor!" Chelsea took in the petite brunette, noting she was dressed to the nines. While her words seemed friendly enough, Chelsea knew a chilly reception when she saw one.

"We were taking advantage of how good the band is tonight." Alex said easily back to the woman. "Chelsea, this is Victoria. She's the chair of the heart ball and our hostess for tonight."

Chelsea returned a fake smile of her own before saying pleasantly enough, "It's a wonderful evening. Quite the event you've pulled off here tonight."

Victoria tilted her head to one side, sizing Chelsea up before adding a simple, "Thank you."

Unexpectedly feeling like a third wheel suddenly, Chelsea announced she needed to visit the ladies room. Victoria turned and pointed towards the grand staircase. "Go to the top of the stairs and to your right."

Chelsea thanked her before glancing at Alex and heading to the stairs. Once she got to the top of the staircase she turned to look at the two of them below her. They seemed deep in conversation, but even from up there Chelsea could see the tension, their body language giving them away. As Victoria turned to move away, Chelsea hurried on her way to the ladies room, curious as to what it was all about.

FIVE

As Chelsea entered the ladies room, she paused to check herself in the mirror. She almost jumped out of her skin when a woman's deep voice spoke to her from a corner of the room. Recovering quickly, Chelsea nodded to the woman's friendly question asking if she were enjoying her evening. Realizing she was an attendant for the ladies room, Chelsea nodded yes, but politely declined her offer for a cigarette, mint, or perfume. She closed the door to her large stall with a decisive click. As she balanced taking care of business with her long dress, she paused briefly when she thought she heard another click.

Chelsea quickly finished her business, prepared to decline the attendant's assistance with washing her hands, not wanting to be pressured to tip her for something she could do for herself. Instead she found herself in an empty room, the attendant gone. After drying her hands, Chelsea checked her lipstick before bending over to shake out her curls and then come back to the mirror. Pleased with what she saw, she headed for the door.

Chelsea had to give the door a hard pull as she went to open it. Thinking it was stuck, she gave it a harder yank. Panic hit her like a ton of bricks as she realized the door was locked and there was no opening it. Frantically she searched for a lock on the inside of the door. She could feel her heart pounding loudly as she tried to force herself to stay calm. She took a minute to collect herself, telling herself she was okay, this was not a big deal. Alex knew where she was and would come look for her sooner or later. Or would he?

"Help! Can someone please help me? The door is locked!" Chelsea started yelling as loudly as she could, trying to keep her hysteria from bubbling to the top. "The door is locked! PLEASE! Someone help me!"

It was happening. Chelsea hadn't been in this place mentally for a long time, but here and now, it was happening. She was desperate NOT to go to that place. She kept telling herself she was okay. They will find me. Someone has a key. Alex will look for me.

"Help me please! Let me out! LET ME OUT NOW! Please someone unlock the door!" Chelsea screamed at the door, pounding on it as hard as she could, begging for someone to open it.

"Chelsea, we're getting the key. Hold on, you'll be out in a minute." Alex's voice came through the door to her a bit muffled, but strong and reassuring.

Chelsea put her hand to her chest, forcing herself to take deep breaths. I'm okay. It's going to be fine. I'm okay. Chelsea kept her pep talk up until she finally heard the key in the lock of the door. She rushed out the door to a small crowd of people, relieved to see Alex's familiar face.

"Chelsea, are you okay? What happened?" Alex asked, his handsome face full of concern.

"I'm okay. I'm fine. But I have to get out of here. I need to leave NOW!" Chelsea said urgently as she headed for the staircase, her green dress flowing behind her.

Alex followed behind her worriedly, calling to her to slow down, not sure how she could move so fast in her heels. Seeing her frantic face, the remaining guests moved out of the way for her as she made a beeline for the door.

She shook her head no when she was asked if she needed a cab, not yet calm enough to stand there and wait for one to be flagged down. She looked up and down the street before turning abruptly and heading in the direction of her hotel.

"Chelsea! Chelsea, wait! Where are you going?" Alex was yelling to her, almost needing to break out in a run to catch up to her.

When he took her arm to stop her, she all but snarled, "Don't touch me!" As she continued speed walking down the street, Alex fell in beside her. He wasn't sure what to say, but chose to walk along beside her. When they finally came to a red light and had to stop, Alex noticed Chelsea give a little shiver in the cool night air.

As he slipped his tux jacket off, he turned to Chelsea and asked quietly, "Would you like my jacket?"

This time when she looked at him he was relieved to see she was calm again. "Yes, thank you."

Alex watched as Chelsea pulled his jacket around herself tightly, seeming to need the security of it. When they reached her hotel, they both paused.

"Do you want to have a last drink Chelsea? Are you okay now?"

She looked like a lost little girl and it took all of Alex's will power not to wrap his arms around her and tell everything was okay.

Chelsea smiled up at Alex. "I'm okay thank you. But I think that I'm not ready to go to my room yet so that would be nice. If you're up for one?"

"Of course." Alex said, returning her smile before he opened the door for her.

Together they walked to their usual spot at the bar, the room mostly empty given the late hour of the night. Alex signaled the bartender, "Two whiskey sours, she'll have Woodford Reserve, please."

Alex pulled a barstool out for Chelsea, but she shook her head. "Do you mind if we sit in a booth?" she asked.

He quickly stretched out his arm, indicating for her to lead the way.

They sat facing each other, Alex waiting to let Chelsea go first. "Sorry about that back there. Not a great end to the evening. I apologize if I embarrassed you."

Alex waited for the bartender to set their drinks down before he spoke. "No worries. I'm sorry that happened to you." Alex paused for a minute before adding. "Are you claustrophobic?" He had seen her face, the sheer terror, and knew it had to be something more than being locked in a bathroom.

Chelsea took a sip of her drink. She wrestled with how much she wanted to share with Alex. She was beyond grateful that he had been there. Even now, sitting with his jacket still around her, she felt relief, comforted by his presence.

"My mom used to lock me in my closet when I was little. She and my dad used to have some pretty gruesome fights. It was her way of protecting me. I haven't been in that place in a long time. I'm glad you were there Alex." Chelsea finally raised her eyes to face him.

Alex took a minute to process what she said. He didn't need a degree in counseling to know it was something. He answered her quietly. "We all have triggers from our past, some of them good and some not so good."

They sat comfortably in the silence, both of them lost in their own thoughts, sipping their bourbons. Chelsea decided it was time to call it a night. As she went to stand, Alex also moved to stand beside her.

"I'll walk you to your room, if that's okay with you?" Alex asked.

Chelsea nodded with a grateful smile.

As they walked through the padded hallways to the Gotham Hotel, Alex asked her casually. "What are you doing tomorrow? Are you a church goer?"

"Umm no. I'll go for my usual run. And then brunch. Any recommendations? I like to treat myself on Sundays." Chelsea tried to be equally casual, hoping he would offer to join her.

She stopped to look at him as they reached her door. "Sarabeth's is my personal favorite. You probably have that somewhere in your notes about me." He said teasingly.

She gave him a brief smile, knowing he didn't mean anything by it. "Good to know, thanks. And thanks again for tonight Alex." She handed him his tux jacket before turning back to unlock her door.

"Chelsea?" As she turned back to him, he pulled her to him, embracing her in a big hug. "I'm here for you. I'll text you my number." He released her reluctantly. As he walked away he suddenly spun around and added, "I'll meet you tomorrow at Sarabeth's. Eleven o'clock. Sharp!"

Chelsea was all smiles as she closed her door behind her, already looking forward to it. She would need the distraction to be able to close her eyes and forget that someone had locked her in a bathroom tonight. She knew in her gut, it hadn't been a fluke, but then who would have done it, and more importantly, why would they bother?

SIX

Employed with Hudson & Butler Publishing for the past couple of months now, Chelsea's ducks were lining up quite nicely. She and Alex were together often in the workplace and out, Chelsea finagling herself into his schedule wherever she could. Although Alex was a good distraction, she was laser focused on her long range plan to get Thomas back in her life, her one true love since they were kids. Katherine Blake, his wife, was an annoying obstacle in her way, but one she had devised a plan for eliminating.

Chelsea had known Thomas since they were children, growing up as neighbors in their affluent neighborhood that bordered the Kansas City Plaza. Despite wanting for nothing in the way of materialistic things, they both emotionally struggled to survive their dysfunctional parents. Thomas had been lucky to have an older sister to turn to for the love and support any child needed to grow up happy and healthy.

Chelsea had not been so lucky as an only child, her mother turning to the bottle to replace the love and support she craved. It took little to provoke her father, who could turn an argument into the most vile of remarks, remarks that would have shattered the strongest of women. It was during those arguments that Chelsea would find herself locked in her room, her mother trying to protect her from the evils of a toxic marriage.

While Thomas's parents faced their own trials in the marriage, they chose to handle their contempt for the other with icy indifference.

Chelsea found this a welcome relief and before she knew it, she was spending more time at Thomas's house than her own. As they grew into teenagers, things took a turn for the worse as Chelsea tried to move their relationship out of the friend zone. When Thomas refused to participate, Chelsea's ugly side came to life, writing in her diary various schemes and plots to manipulate Thomas into doing what she wanted.

She had been devastated when he had gone to college in Columbia, leaving her high and dry on the UMKC campus. She made a commitment to herself to work hard and get a degree that would grant her some financial independence as an adult. As she worked her way through four years of classes and numerous preppy college boys, she realized she was more like her father than she thought. She wasn't afraid to hustle and be her own sugar daddy. But still, she had assumed when college was done and Thomas came back, he would fall for the woman she had grown into.

It was during one of the annual ski trips that she found herself sorely mistaken. Apparently Thomas had graduated with more than a degree in engineering, but also found the love of his life, some small town girl Chelsea could only hate. She had lost her shit when she learned Thomas had proposed and she would not be the first Mrs. Thomas Bell after all.

Never one to turn to alcohol like her mother, Chelsea had relied on cocaine to dull her heartache, and allowed her to get on with the business of adulting. With her degree in business, she had found a job working for a literary agency. The process of taking an author's idea and getting it into print appealed to Chelsea. Since she was a little girl, she had used reading as a means to escape the harsh realities of her life and being the bookworm she was, the job had actually been a good fit for her. She felt productive and successful in her assignments and paid attention to the fine print, learning everything she could.

But still, she wanted a man in her life to wine and dine her and quite by accident, met her first husband. He was handsome even for an old goat and knew how to make Chelsea feel special. While he was handsome and rich enough for the greediest of bitches, Chelsea quickly discovered she was nothing more than a trophy wife or a booty call at best. Bored with her choice, she had stupidly strayed from the marriage and found herself served divorce papers and not a penny to her name. This time there wasn't enough cocaine in the world to numb her self-induced pain.

Having hit rock bottom one night, Chelsea decided Thomas and Kat were the reason her life sucked as much as it did. She became obsessed with finding a way to ruin their lives like they had ruined hers. As with everything she did, Chelsea hatched a plan and went all in. She had researched Cat's past, finding an unsavory old boyfriend who was currently serving time. Naively she had reached out to him and formed a tenuous partnership to destroy Cat and Thomas.

Chelsea had been delighted when she had read Cat's article about the traditional way to publish a book versus self publishing. She took it as a sign that this was her ticket to manipulating Thomas and Cat's relationship to the point their marriage could fall apart before her eyes. It had taken her only a week to empty her large closet, her clothes packed and ready for her move to New York City. She had cashed in on some stocks to have some money in her account, but would mostly be relying on credit and her family name until she was once again employed and making bank.

Chelsea soon discovered Kat had already left her manuscript with Alex's secretary, her interview with Alex more of a way in the door at Hudson & Butler rather than yet another article for the Washington Post where Kat was employed. Chelsea had begrudgingly given her props for that, admiring any woman who wasn't afraid to go big. After getting hired by Alex himself as a junior editor, Chelsea had made it her mission to be the one to handle Kat's manuscript, hoping it actually was good enough for someone to sign off on for publication.

It had taken only a couple of days for Chelsea to find Kat's manuscript in the slush pile and secure her as a client. Chelsea would always cherish the look on her face when she realized Chelsea would be her editor. It had been an expensive meeting, as Chelsea had used her personal funds to give Kat a nice "advance" and lure her into signing her contract. She had worked hard to keep her satisfied smile to herself as she sent Kat off with a bottle of champagne and just enough time to catch the train back to DC.

Having her ducks in a row gave Chelsea a sense of having control over her life again, giving her time to focus her attention on Alex. Despite her best efforts, it had taken more than she anticipated to get Alex to sleep with her after signing her contract. Alex surprised her by turning out to be a pretty decent human despite being a man with a lot of money and power. From the first time they met, she had felt a strong physical attraction to Alex, but the way he had taken care of her the night of the Heart Ball had tugged at her emotionally as well. She was more than happy to let him wine and dine her, taking time to get to know her before they slept together.

Coming out of her mental reminiscing, Chelsea resumed her focus on Kat's calendar of author visits she had arranged around the states. In the next six months she had scheduled thirteen visits, hoping Kat wouldn't know if she were coming or going and in turn putting a strain on her and Thomas's relationship. She was impressed that Kat had mostly held her own in their initial meeting, although she was no match for Chelsea's master plan.

She appreciated that Kat was thirsty for her new book to become a New York Times Bestseller and Chelsea was there to make it happen. Following plenty of well known authors on social media, she knew book tours were a way to sell books and therefore necessary for Kat to participate in as well. Like her, Chelsea could only assume Kat was willing to do whatever it took to make her dreams come true. Actually, Chelsea realized she was counting on it.

SEVEN

Chelsea checked her watch, deciding she was starving and it was time to call it a day. Alex had mentioned earlier he had a business meeting for dinner and would be out late. With a smile on her face Chelsea decided to head to his apartment and surprise him when he got home.

Her first hurdle was getting the door person to buzz her in. She pretended to dig in her bag, assuming they were watching her. She knew most of the night staff as she and Alex had been in and out of the building together several times. She regretted that tonight's door person was a woman, knowing she could manipulate a man much easier.

Finally she gave up pretending to look and hit the talk button with an exasperated voice. "Hey Samantha, can you help me out? It's Samantha right? I changed purses this morning and just realized I forgot to switch over my key fob Alex gave me. He's in a late meeting and asked me to meet him here. Do you mind buzzing me in? I'm happy to call Alex so you can hear for yourself."

Chelsea crossed her fingers behind her back hoping her bluff would work. She always made a point to know the door people as you never knew when it could come in handy. Samantha seemed nonplussed by her theatrics, but buzzed her in just the same.

"Thanks Samantha! You're the best!" Chelsea pretended to gush. She was all smiles as the elevator whisked her up to the penthouse. Luckily she had secretly made a copy of Alex's key a few weeks ago.

Chelsea didn't hesitate to make herself at home, going to the kitchen to grab her leftover salad and salmon she knew was there from dinner last night. She poured herself a half glass of wine before heading to the bedroom. She had grabbed another manuscript from the slush pile on her way out of the office and would get some reading done while she waited for Alex to get home. Kicking her shoes off, Chelsea stepped out of her dress and into one of Alex's shirts before she climbed into the cozy king sized bed and settled in.

Arranging the pillows behind her, she took a minute to inhale the smell Alex left behind. Even without him there, she hungered for him, easily imagining his strong capable body in bed beside her. Their first time together had been only a few weeks ago, but well worth the wait. She closed her eyes, letting the memory of it wash over her.

She had been working late, assuming she was the only one there. She had gone to the bathroom to freshen up before she headed to The Reading Room, hoping Alex would be there. As soon as she stepped from the bathroom and into the hallway, it had become a laser show, the alarms ringing loudly in her ears. She panicked and ran to the front of the office, trying to remember her code. Suddenly Alex had thrown open the door, his handsome face concerned and then surprised to see her there.

Quickly he had disarmed the alarm and turned to her. "I just checked your office and you weren't in it. I thought you left." he said.

Chelsea frowned, "I just went to the ladies room. I didn't realize you were still here. Why were you looking for me?"

He paused before admitting, "I was hoping we could go for a drink. Or see if you wanted to grab a late dinner. Or just hang out at my place. It's Friday night and I thought we could let work go and enjoy ourselves."

Chelsea felt herself start to warm as he walked up to her, his body close enough to kiss her. "I just have a few things to finish up and then I'm down for anything," she said.

His finger lightly traced first her cheek, then over her jawbone, before moving to her lips. "Anything?" he asked softly.

Her eyes were locked into his. "Anything." she repeated. "Will you come with me while I get my things?"

He held his hand out indicating she should lead the way. She smiled to herself knowing he was enjoying the view of her backside. She closed her laptop and packed her bag, her movements deliberate, knowing he was watching her.

"I'm ready when you are." she said.

He walked over to her and took her face in his hands. "You are the most interesting, beautiful woman I've ever met. I've been patient, but tonight's the night." Then he kissed her so long and deep her knees almost buckled.

He had her undressed in no time, their clothes all over the floor. He kissed her gently at first but had quickly become more urgent as her hand massaged him. He led her to her couch and she lay down all smiles. Never had she had to wait so long for a man to take her nor had she ever felt such a strong physical attraction like she did to Alex. Coming out of her reverie, she sighed heavily as she picked up a manuscript and pushed up her glasses. There would be time for that later.

Voices woke Chelsea, bringing her out of a deep sleep. Her empty wine glass and salad bowl sat beside the bedside lamp, the soft glow of it the only light in the darkened room. Abruptly she sat up, wide awake as she realized one of the voices was a woman's. She could hear Alex talking, his voice calm and deliberate. Had he brought his business meeting home after dinner? Chelsea's heart was pounding as she got out of bed and walked over to the closed door to listen better. Damn these well made doors.

She could tell by the woman's tone she wasn't happy, but Chelsea could not make out what she was saying. Frantically Chelsea went back to the bed, doing a quick inventory that she had brought everything into the room with her. She stood deliberating if she should put her dress back on or climb into bed, following through on her original plan to surprise Alex.

Suddenly the door swung open. Alex letting his frame fill the doorway, his arms crossed over his chest. Chelsea could see he was not amused to see her standing there. Putting her hands on her hips, she decided to play offense.

"You never told me your meeting was with a woman tonight!" Chelsea said, realizing she actually felt as annoyed as she sounded.

"That's because my meeting is my business. How did you get in here anyway? Even if you talked Samantha into buzzing you in, I know I left my door locked this morning." Alex's eyes had narrowed as he thought through how she had managed it.

Suddenly he moved to pick her bag up out of the chair, digging furiously for the key he assumed she must have. "What the hell? How is it that you have your own key to my penthouse?"

Not giving her time to answer, he picked up her dress and threw it at her. "You need to go. It's been a long day and I need to go to bed." He could see Chelsea thinking about how she wanted to play her cards and added loudly, "NOW!"

"Okay, okay! I'm sorry I didn't think it would be a big deal! I just wanted to surprise you!" Chelsea was trying her best to sell it, but quickly realized he was in no mood to be distracted by a romp in the hay.

After getting back into her dress, Chelsea threw the manuscript in her bag and gathered the rest of her things. Alex followed her to the door, his face grim as he opened it for her.

"I'm really sorry Alex." Chelsea mumbled as she walked out the door. She jumped as Alex loudly shut the door behind her, just short of a slam.

Chelsea mentally chastised herself all the way down to the first floor. She tried to decide if she had gotten so full of herself she hadn't even thought through the idea of how Alex would see it or was he just in a mood and overreacting?

When Samantha saw her get off the elevator, she picked up her phone and called for a cab without even asking. Chelsea was surprised when Samantha rattled off her address.

Seeing her look of surprise Samantha said dryly. "Yeah I make it a point to know everybody in and out of this building and I knew it wasn't going to fly for you to be up there on your own. Now you know it too."

Chelsea did not appreciate how smug Samantha was, but thanked her just the same as she went outside to meet her cab. Climbing into the back seat, it occurred to her she had overstepped Alex's morale compass, his much stronger than her own. As the cab pulled away from the curb, she was already wondering what she could do to get Alex to forgive her? It never occurred to her that he wouldn't.

EIGHT

It had been almost a month since Chelsea had actually laid eyes on Alex. She had needed to focus on why she had wanted to get hired with Hudson & Butler to begin with, and all the free time gave her plenty of time to do so. She had made a "family emergency" trip to take care of one of the balls she was currently juggling in her masterplan. Despite how well things were going with Kat and marketing her book, Chelsea had not felt great about the other half of her masterplan, her visit to the prison to meet Kat's old boyfriend leaving her with a bad taste in her mouth. She was no angel by any means, but seeing his face and the hard glint in his eyes left Chelsea feeling they might all be in danger. She had tried to renege on their arrangement, but he refused unless she wanted to write him a million dollar check. Sadly this was not an option for her.

Only time would tell and Chelsea knew it would be a miracle if all her balls fell into place as she planned. She kept her eyes on the prize, which was of course being reunited with Thomas, her childhood crush, after having successfully pushed Kat out of his life. For as long as she could remember she had wanted to be Mrs. Thomas Bell. She was convinced her happiness lay in all his famly's wealth and the entitlement the Bell name could bring her. She had put a lot of balls in motion at a very hefty price tag and now was not the time to be so worried about Alex.

Chelsea had learned the hard way that Alex was not quick to forgive. His secretary had a plethora of excuses for her in or out of the office and Chelsea grew more frustrated as the excuses piled up. He was unavailable, he was in a meeting, he couldn't be disturbed, he was out of town, he was working from home, etc. He most definitely was not taking her calls or texts.

Feeling frustrated and bored one Friday afternoon, Chelsea resorted to reaching out to the other junior editors around her. As they approached quitting time, Chelsea propped herself on the edge of someone's desk and asked in her friendliest voice, "Who knows a good place to go for happy hour?"

As two or three of them exchanged looks between themselves, Chelsea quickly offered, "Drinks on me to the first one recommending the winning place for happy hour!"

Within an hour there were six junior editors squished into a booth at none other than The Reading Room. Chelsea had been a mixture of excited disbelief and trepidation at the thought Alex might already be there. To her relief he was not seated at the bar in their usual spot. She tried to relax and get to know the people around her better, although to be honest, there might not be enough tequila in the world to make that bearable. Their topics of conversation ranged from sports to the latest episode of The Bachelor to dissecting Obamacare and how it would or would not work for them.

Chelsea was just about to excuse herself and head home when the table suddenly became quiet. As she finished her drink, she looked up to see Alex standing in front of their table. "Hey there Mr. Butler! TGIF! Care to join us?" the newest and overly ambitious editor offered.

Chelsea watched in amusement as Alex stumbled on what to say, trying not to be dismissive nor get himself tangled into their happy hour shenanigans. Suddenly she caught her breath as his eyes met hers. He lingered a little too long giving Chelsea all the hope she needed.

"TGIF!" Alex reluctantly responded. "How did you all end up here?"

"Well, Chelsea was looking for a good place for happy hour and Frankie had been here before on a date and said she thought it was a pretty cool place, so here we are. And it is right around the corner from the office. Have you been here before Mr. Butler?" the kid replied.

Chelsea was riveted to see what Alex would say. "Maybe once or twice. The drinks are pretty pricey."

"Oh Chelsea offered to buy us the first round!" Damn, this kid clearly did not know when to quit!

Once again Alex's eyes were on her, his expression impossible to read. "Did she now. Enjoy that. Have a good weekend." he said before he walked away.

One of the senior editors smacked the kid on the back of his head. "What are you thinking? You invited the CEO to join us for happy hour!"

"Hey! The man likes a good drink as much as we do!" They all turned to watch Alex order from the bartender as he pulled up a stool.

"What do you think he drinks?" someone else wondered aloud.

"Who cares?! Have you guys heard the real story? Apparently he's sleeping with one of our junior editors!"

Chelsea held her breath as someone else waved her off. "Nah, that's old news. I heard he's already moved on."

As someone suddenly announced that it was after eight, the group instantly started making excuses why they should head home. Chelsea joined them, hanging at the back as they headed to the door. She was almost out when she realized she had 'forgot' her bag. Surprisingly one of them offered to wait for her so she didn't have to walk alone.

She thanked the kid before adding, "That's okay, I'll see you on Monday!" She was confident he had no idea of her intentions as she headed back into the bar, half wondering if Alex was expecting her.

She retrieved her bag from under the bench in their booth, right where she had stashed it ten minutes ago. She didn't hem or haw but pushed her way through the groups of people scattered around, heading straight to the bar where Alex sat sipping his whiskey sour.

"Is this stool taken?" she asked him lightly.

He hesitated, taking a sip of his drink before he even looked at her. "Apparently not."

Chelsea didn't wait for him to invite her to sit down, almost certain he would not. She signaled the bartender before adding, "I'll have what he's having with Woodford Reserve please."

"This seems familiar," he said dryly.

"We need to talk and move past this. We work together." Chelsea said forcefully.

Alex turned on his barstool to look at her. "What could you possibly say to make the situation better?"

"Go ahead Alex. Tell me off. I deserve it. I crossed a line." When Alex sat staring into his drink with nothing to say, Chelsea pressed on. "Go ahead, say it! You don't know how you're ever going to trust me again. Alex! Can you please be a grown up and talk to me for a minute?"

Finally he turned to look at her again. She shrank from what she saw in his eyes, a mixture of pity and disappointment. "You're right Chelsea. I don't know how I'm going to trust you again. I'm trying to figure out WHY you would go to such lengths."

Chelsea could feel herself tensing, mentally trying to choose between flight or fight. Should she just walk away? If her calendar went according to plan, she would only be at Hudson & Butler for another month or so anyway. It was a big office and it should be easy for them to continue avoiding each other. Chelsea shook her head, knowing she had never backed down from a fight before. Besides, she had spent too many sleepless nights rehearsing what she would say to Alex.

"Alex, I don't know what got into me." She decided to start there.

"Strike one. Try again. We both know you are tenacious with a plan, remember?"

"Alright, you're right. Here's the truth. Do you remember that day you had me go to your apartment and get you a new shirt and tie? You spilled a bowl of soup or something and you had a meeting you needed to prep for. That's when you gave me your key to get in. On my way back to the office, I stopped by a hardware store and had a copy of your key made. I just thought we had something real and our relationship was headed in that direction."

"Strike two. You were closer that time, but as I recall you offered to go and get me a new shirt and tie. Last chance." His eyes were narrowed at her.

Chelsea took a sip of her drink, taken aback at how well Alex was able to see through her. It was time to put her cards on the table. "You're right Alex. I saw an opportunity and I took it and ran. I don't have a good reason for doing it. I can't apologize enough and I wish more than anything we could go back to where we were. I made a stupid mistake and I can't begin to tell you how much I regret it!"

"Because?" Alex asked. When he saw her puzzled look he pressed on. "You regret it because why?"

Chelsea went all in. "I regret it because I made a mistake, I dropped my guard and didn't think something through. I regret it because I messed up a good thing with the only friend I have in this city. And I regret it because it kills me to see the disappointment in your eyes. And I miss you." Chelsea looked away first, reaching for her bourbon to comfort her. As she said the words, she realized just how much she really did miss Alex.

"Wow! I think I believe you." Alex said softly. "Telling the truth is really hard for you, isn't it?"

Suddenly Chelsea jumped off her barstool, deciding she was done. She opened her bag and pulled out a twenty dollar bill she threw down on the bar for her drink. As she headed for the door, she decided she had one more thing to say to Alex. "I don't need you to patronize me

Alex!" She snapped. "This feels awful! If you can't forgive me, then you can't forgive me. But it will be your loss!"

Chelsea was surprised to realize she was close to tears and that pissed her off even more. Chelsea did NOT cry over anything, ever. Yelling, bitching, manipulating and occasionally faked hysteria, yes to all the above, but crying, absolutely not! Angrily she pushed the door open, walking out to signal for a cab. As she reached to open the cab door, Alex was suddenly beside her, opening it for her. Warily she climbed into the back seat, not sure of his intention. She was even more surprised when he motioned for her to scoot over and he climbed into the cab as well, giving the driver his address rather than hers.

Chelsea sat stiffly looking out the window, as far away from him as possible, enduring the silently painful ride to his building. Chelsea was thoroughly confused when he got out and then stood holding the door for her, clearly expecting her to get out too. Seeing her hesitation he held his hand out to her.

"Aren't you coming?" he asked, his words borderline friendly.

Chelsea's first instinct was to decline, but reluctantly she gave him her hand, his touch sending a jolt through her. Without a word she followed behind him, nodding to the person at the front desk, thankful it wasn't Samantha sitting there. Once they were in the privacy of Alex's penthouse, she turned to him.

"What the hell am I doing here Alex?" she stood with her hands on her hips, glaring at him.

Catching her by surprise, Alex was suddenly reaching for her, pulling her close, embracing her in a hug. Chelsea had a flash to the night of the heart ball. She tried to resist his good smells, his strong arms around her, his face nuzzled into her neck.

"God I've missed you!" Suddenly he pulled away, running his hands through his hair. Realizing he was already second guessing his decision, Chelsea made a move of her own.

She went to him, putting her arms around his neck, pulling his face down to hers before she took his lips hostage, pressing her entire body against him. She willingly let him spread her lips open, his tongue hungrily sweeping her mouth and even more willingly she wrapped her legs around him as he picked her up and carried her to the bedroom. In record time they lay naked in his bed, their bodies rediscovering their favorite parts of the other.

Before long they lay wrapped around each other, in an emotionally exhausted heap of satisfaction. Chelsea used her well manicured finger to make circles on his chest, enjoying the feel of his skin. Softly she said, "I am sorry Alex. I promise I'll never try to manipulate you again. And for the record, I missed you more."

Alex laughed before pulling her on top of him, bringing her face close to his. "I accept your apology and for the record, you better mean that. I spent too many years being manipulated by my ex-wife and I will not go there again. Fool me once, shame on you. Fool me twice, shame on me."

She was surprised to hear his admission to having an ex, but was more focused on something else. Fairly certain she knew the answer, Chelsea stupidly asked anyway. "I promise, no more stupid stuff. But what happens for fool me a third time?"

Alex's eyes narrowed slightly before he said grimly. "You don't want to know." She believed him, crossing her fingers it would never come to that. Chelsea's record wasn't the best and she did have this masterplan going. For once Chelsea wished she was a religious person, knowing she most definitely should be saying a prayer.

NINE

It had taken no time for Chelsea and Alex to fall back into their old ways, although Chelsea made a point to tread lightly. The pace at work was picking up as more clients were assigned to her, leaving little time for hanky panky at the office. She was always willing and able to go to Alex's place whatever the time and if he didn't offer, she would offer her place. Occasionally they both agreed they needed a night to themselves and Chelsea found herself in bed early with a new manuscript from the slush pile to read.

Her master plan seemed on track, but she was definitely having second thoughts. She worried about the part of her plan that concerned Thomas. Looking back, she realized what a bad place she had been in to have hatched such a vindictive plan to begin with.

She was fairly certain she had made a big mistake in digging into Kat's past and giving a certain someone the tools to make her and Thomas's lives hell. The old boyfriend was out of prison now, their meetings always making Chelsea uncomfortable. She often walked away from them hoping she wasn't as mentally unbalanced as he was. More than once, she had tried to call off their deal, but he would have none of it, reminding her she would need to write him a million dollar check for that to happen. Knowing that was impossible, Chelsea let the plan roll, hoping for the best.

Kat's sales for her book were going very well and Chelsea was happy to take most of the credit for her success. She had reminded Kat more than once that just because you can write a book, doesn't mean you know how to sell it. She loved that Kat needed her, making her putty in her hands.

It was late in the day when a knock on her door caused Chelsea to look up from what she was reading, her reply short. "Yes? Come in."

She smiled at the sight of Alex. "Well aren't you a pleasant surprise!"

Alex walked to her desk, tossing the folder in his hand to the middle of her desk. "Tell me about this."

Without even looking at it, Chelsea knew it was her budget for Kat's grand finale in her book tour. She had arranged for a red carpet event at The Spy Museum in Washington DC. Knowing it was Kat and Thomas's current hometown, she was expecting a major turnout.

"What do you want to know? It's going to be an epic night and should be the final push to get Kat onto the New York Times Best Sellers list." Chelsea said matter of factly.

"An epic night with a hefty price tag. We're not hosting a small wedding are we?" Alex asked, seeming seriously concerned.

Chelsea got out of her chair and came around to sit on the edge of her desk, perching herself in front of Alex. "I've always been taught you have to spend money to make money. Are you telling me Hudson & Butler can't afford this?"

Alex crossed his arms across his chest, his face serious. "This is highly unusual to host an event for any author at this price tag. What's so important about Katherine Blake?"

Chelsea took a minute, trying to decide quickly how much to share with Alex. Would it be better to be honest or worse for getting her budget approved. She deflected, needing time to think.

"I'm sorry Alex. I guess I didn't realize that there's a standard budget for our book events. What would be a budget you would approve?" she asked.

Alex narrowed his eyes before he said, "Answer the question Chelsea. What's the deal with Katherine Blake?"

She took a deep breath, choosing her words carefully. "Kat is married to my dearest friend Thomas Bell. We grew up together and we go way back. She's the one who interviewed you for the Washington Post article." She tried to keep her voice casual. "I have to admit I do have a personal interest in Kat and her book doing well."

When Alex failed to respond, Chelsea pressed on. "But this event is a rare opportunity to partner with a space that fits the book. Kat was inspired to write this story while walking through The Spy Museum, writing a historical fiction about one of our first and most successful female spies during WWII."

She could see Alex still wasn't convinced. "The museum is giving us the space for free. You're paying for food and entertainment and it's a cash bar. The red carpet is to ensure there will be plenty of publicity for free. I promise we will sell enough books to pay the tab at the end of the night. But if you like, you can chat with Kat about it over dinner tonight. She's due in my office any minute for a meeting." Chelsea threw the ball into Alex's court, having only one more argument up her sleeve. She was relieved when he finally acquiesced.

"Against my better judgment I'm going to trust you Chelsea. It sounds like a great idea, but you should know if we pay the tab on an event like this for one author, others will expect the same for their books."

Seeing how serious Alex was, she walked up close to him, her eyes locked into his. She put her hand on his arm as she said, "You can trust me when I say this event will pay for itself." She paused for only a minute before turning on her heel abruptly, returning to her perch on the end of her desk. "Kat is the one paying the tab with every sale of her book. She's worked hard and deserves this finale for her book tour."

They both turned at the discreet sound of an "ahem." Kat was standing in the doorway, hesitant to interrupt them, but not wanting to appear to be eavesdropping. "Am I interrupting? Your secretary wasn't at her desk so I wandered in."

Chelsea gave Kat a big smile. "Come in Kat! I was just telling Alex you were due for a meeting and invited him to join us for dinner tonight." Both women turned to Alex for a confirmation.

"Actually I'm going to leave you ladies to it. Congratulations on the success of your book Katherine. Chelsea assures me you are headed to that list you're after. Enjoy your dinner tonight." As he talked he was casually moving to the door, ready to exit.

He was almost out the door when Chelsea called him back. "Oh Alex! I think you forgot something?" He turned to see her holding a pen out to him, the budget waiting to be signed. Without a word, he quickly signed it and left.

"Thank you!" she called after him as he closed her office door, Kat the only one there to witness her smug smile. It was going to be a great night and Chelsea was excited for Kat to see what she had planned for her, although she was certain she would enjoy the outcome way more than Kat would.

TEN

Her oversized suitcase sat on the floor mostly packed and ready for the red carpet event in Washington DC tomorrow night. She was home alone tonight as her flight was ridiculously bright and early in the morning. There were things to be done before show time and Chelsea hated being rushed. Her body was tired having added an extra mile to her run today, trying to ensure she would sleep tonight. However, her mind bounced around refusing to land and let her go to sleep.

Chelsea was impatient to lay eyes on Thomas tomorrow. It had been way too long and she tried to ignore the wiggle of doubt that any of it would go according to plan. She had gone through numerous dresses before she had found the perfect one, desperate for Thomas to give her a second look. She couldn't deny Kat cleaned up well, but the curves and attitude they would each bring to their look, were like comparing sparkling wine to champagne and rather pointless.

She had to admit Kat had seemed a little uptight over dinner, talking about Thomas, but not overly. They had both been pleased at the great turn out for her author visit at the Greenlight Bookstore in Brooklyn on Saturday. It made Chelsea smile to remember Kat's appreciation for the car service only to find her already sitting in the back seat. She had relaxed when Chelsea handed her a glass of champagne, toasting Kat's success and the near end of her author tour.

Her expression had been just what she hoped for as Chelsea announced she would be in DC for her event the next weekend. It was then her suspicions had been confirmed, Kat had never told Thomas she was working with Chelsea. Oh how sweet it was to imagine how this conversation would play out in the Bell home. Chelsea refused to dwell on the fact that she was probably Thomas's least favorite person in the world, having manipulated him countless times as they navigated high school together. It surprised her to realize she would be good either way. Old habits were hard to break, but there was definitely someone new on her radar.

It made Chelsea smile just to think of Alex. She could picture him in bed, propped up on his layers of pillows, his reading glasses on, his latest book choice resting on his smooth six pack, his hair unruly as it tended to be at the end of a long day. As much as she tried to keep the upper hand, Alex had a hold of her and she wasn't sure where it was headed.

Before she knew it, Chelsea was busy enjoying the respectable number of guests milling about The Spy Museum. She knew Kat and Thomas had just arrived and she wanted to be just a step behind them on the red carpet. More than anything she wanted to see a picture of herself with Thomas and Kat in the social pages of the paper tomorrow morning. Her satisfaction was short-lived though when Thomas moved off the red carpet as soon as he saw her. Ignoring her disappointment, she called Kat's name like a long lost friend and went to stand beside her, all smiles.

When Kat allowed only one picture before walking away too, Chelsea forced herself to remain calm, trying to keep her bright red lipstick in the form of a smile. Suddenly the small group of photographers parted ways, and she was surprised to see Alex walking towards her, a smile on his handsome face. The sight of him in a tux took her breath away, but she felt nothing but gratitude as he came to stand beside her on the red carpet, his arm casually draped around her waist. They had not once talked about him coming and yet here he was. It wasn't out of line given the magnitude of this event and the fact that he was the Butler of Hudson & Butler.

The evening moved along quickly, everyone enjoying the event and all the fanfare that went with it. Chelsea had planned to approach Thomas when Kat was busy signing books, but Alex had intervened. Reluctantly she followed his suggestion to go and check on food and entertainment, knowing they were the two things Alex had actually had to sign off on for the night. Before she knew it everyone had settled into the main room, the drinks and hors d'oeuvres flowing, the band inspiring people to dance.

As Thomas and Kat went to the dance floor, Chelsea once again attempted to intervene only to be whisked away by Alex. She had turned to him in frustration, demanding to be let go. Into her ear he quickly reminded her she was hosting a very expensive event and would remain in a professional capacity as such, putting her damn personal agenda away if she didn't want to be fired. The force of his words brought her up abruptly as they moved around the dance floor, doubting he would ever really fire her. Or would he?

ELEVEN

The tension in the car to their hotel had been palatable and Chelsea stood waiting for Alex to open their hotel door before she would start making up for what she had done. She wasn't exactly sure why he was annoyed with her, but she was pretty sure she knew of a way to help him get over it.

Chelsea stood by the closed door, watching as Alex laid his Tuxedo jacket on the back of a chair. He stood looking at her as he took off his tie and proceeded to unbutton his shirt. Chelsea decided she would play dumb, like nothing was amiss. She went to stand in front of Alex, reaching for the button on his pants.

"Have I told you how handsome you looked in your tux tonight? It meant so much to me when you joined me on the red carpet tonight. Thank you for being here." Chelsea said seductively.

Alex's face was hard, his eyes dark. "You didn't need to say a word. Your actions told me how much you enjoyed having me there beside you."

Getting a hint of why Alex was angry, Chelsea was quick to pacify him. "Aww Alex, you already knew I was there to support my friends, Kat and Thomas. But enough about them, let me show you now how much I appreciate you being here."

Chelsea had Alex's pants down to the floor, which he stepped out of and laid on top of his jacket. He shook off his shirt and watched to see what Chelsea would do next. He watched as she unzipped her own dress, letting it fall down around her ankles. She was relieved to see Alex's reaction to her nakedness. As she moved toward him, he took a step in the direction of the bathroom.

"Not tonight Chelsea. I'm tired and ready to sleep." He said gruffly.

Chelsea moved to stand between him and the bathroom. "I don't think your body knows what your mouth is saying." she said. He grabbed her arm when she reached for him.

"I said not tonight Chelsea!" Alex said forcefully.

Keeping her eyes locked into his, Chelsea reached again, refusing to take no for an answer. She heard him moan as she moved her hand over him. He pushed her away from him.

"You want it, fine, go lay on the bed." Alex barked hoarsely

Chelsea was stunned by the force with which Alex entered her, his anger clear. There was no tenderness, no foreplay, nothing. Having pushed him into it, she knew she couldn't ask him to stop. Laying there under him, she suddenly realized why Alex was so angry.

She was surprised when Alex stopped and looked at her. "Are you crying?" he asked, rolling off of her immediately.

Chelsea had not even realized she was until he asked. She quickly wiped the tears before she turned to him, his eyes not able to meet hers.

"I'm sorry. I shouldn't have been so rough. I don't know what came over me." he said to her.

Laying her hand on his arm, Chelsea said softly, "I do and I'm the one who should be sorry."

"For what?" he asked gruffly, laying his arm across his eyes.

"I know I hurt you. When I saw you walking up to me on the red carpet, you took my breath away. But then stupidly I chose to chase someone else when you were right there in front of me. I hurt you and I'm sorry. You really care about me, don't you?" The surprise in her voice wasn't lost on him.

Alex looked at Chelsea, his face unreadable. Why was he so damn hard to read? She rolled back to her back, feeling her face heating up.

What was she thinking? How could someone like Alex really care about her? Gently he took her arm off her face and rolled her back to face him.

"Of course I care about you Chelsea, probably more than I should, why else would I be here? Do you think it's just for the sex? And you did hurt me, but I shouldn't have been so. . .so. . .rough."

This time Chelsea recognized tears were sliding down her face. Looking concerned, Alex pulled her to him, his arms engulfing her, her face pressed to his chest. "Why are you crying now?"

"No one's ever cared about me before Alex. Not really cared about me! You deserve someone way better than me! Someone not broken, someone who knows how to love you back." Chelsea said, her voice sad.

Alex was taken aback by what Chelsea was saying, the reality of it sinking in. He was startled to realize she wasn't trying to be dramatic, but believed it to be true. Alex pushed her away just enough to look at her, his dark eyes boring into hers. "Chelsea I can't be the first person to care about you!" When she shook her head, he asked softly, "What about your family?"

She pulled away from him, unable to look him in the face. "My father thought I was a waste of his sperm and belittled my mother for it every time they fought. He hated us both."

Alex tried like hell to keep the shock and dismay from his face, cringing inwardly when Chelsea glanced at him. His family had always been close, even as they all became adults and started to create their own lives. He couldn't imagine growing up like Chelsea had. It was then he remembered her reaction to being locked in the bathroom, a trigger from her childhood she said when her parents would have fights.

Alex pulled her to him, his arms wrapping around her tightly. "You deserve happiness Chelsea and people who care about you. I'll always be here for you. I want to be the reason you're happy and I'll be there to catch you when you fall. You can count on me."

Chelsea pulled away to search his face, trying to decide if he was telling her the truth. Without even thinking about it she said, "But you said I don't want to know what happens if I get three strikes. We both know tonight was strike two! Alex, you know I'm going to get another strike and then what? You're done caring about me?"

Alex knew she had a point. He pulled her to him again. "That was stupid I said that, Chelsea. If you mess up, I'm still going to care about you. A lot, I promise. You can trust me, Chelsea."

He kissed the top of her head, regretting he had ever said that, hating to admit she had a valid point. He had insinuated three strikes and he was done. The truth was he more than cared for Chelsea, he was in love with her. He appreciated her honesty too, nervously believing her when she said she would mess up again, but having a better understanding of why. All he could do was hope it wouldn't be life altering.

TWELVE

Nervously Chelsea gulped down the rest of her coffee, her stomach not able to handle anything solid. Her body was on high alert knowing today was the day of reckoning. She had slept very little last night, dreading the nightmare that was going to be put in motion in a couple of hours. After months of planning, preparing, and manipulating, Chelsea's plan was finally going to come to fruition today. Chelsea knew what she had to do.

Grimly she left her hotel room, her ear pods playing loudly as she headed out for a run to clear her head. There was no turning back this horrible plan she had put into play, but she could warn Thomas and Kat about what was to come. It probably wasn't going to help, but she had to try. After all, she really did love Thomas and surprisingly, had come to care about Kat too.

Too quickly she found herself knocking on their door, knowing she was just a few minutes ahead of him. Hearing the elevator ding again, she checked the hallway to make sure he wasn't early. She wasn't feeling great about the plan she had hatched during her run, but at this point it was all she had.

She was curious as to if Kat and Thomas had figured out who he really was, assuming they had compared notes sooner or later. Whatever happened, she hoped they would never realize she was the one to put this plan in motion. As Kat opened the door, she promised herself she would find a way to make this right, whatever the cost.

It didn't take long for her plan to go up in smoke, the three of them at the mercy of the gun he waved around. Chelsea and Kat had been dismissed to the bank, retrieving his million dollars. Chelsea could only hope this nightmare was soon to finish as she sat the heavy bag of money on the kitchen bar. It annoyed the hell out of her that she had been forced to go to the bank and withdraw the money to make him happy. It had been even more devastating to have to call Alex and ask him for it. Hearing the anger and disbelief in his voice, she knew he had never expected for strike three to occur so soon nor be so expensive.

She watched the crazy man warily, dismayed to see he was still waving his gun around, yet relieved to see Thomas seemed to be hanging in there. The three of them moved back to Thomas's office as he demanded, all of them leery of the gun and his unbalanced mental state. It all happened quickly, his gun suddenly raised at Thomas, Chelsea throwing herself between him and the gun, feeling the pain as a bullet ripped into her gut. She felt herself fall to the floor, the loud thud ringing in her ears before everything went black. This had never been part of her plan.

THIRTEEN

It had been months since that fateful day at Kat and Thomas's apartment. After her near death experience, Chelsea found herself a different person and happier than she had ever been in her life. Stupidly, desperately she had masterminded the mother of all mess ups and inflicted it on people she actually cared about. She had been shocked to find they had forgiven her as she lay in a hospital bed, her gunshot wound taking a life or death toll on her body. Instinctively she had taken a bullet for Thomas that day, bringing her to a crossroads in her life in more ways than one.

Alex had not hesitated to become her caregiver and she would be forever grateful to him for bringing her into his home. His gentle touch as he changed her bandages daily, melted Chelsea's heart. He had personally taken her to PT, but once he learned her routines, had taken it upon himself to supervise her workouts in his home gym. He had made sure all her needs were met and for the first time in her life, Chelsea knew how it felt to be cared for and loved by someone. She was falling hard for Alex and she could only hope he felt the same.

Chelsea had put the brutal chapter behind her, yet another ugly story from her past, but grateful for the much needed change it had forced upon her. For once in her life, Chelsea was trying her hardest to be the best version of herself, to choose happiness, and to maybe even believe there could be a happily ever after in her future after all.

She came out of her reverie as Alex squeezed her hand, quick to flash him a smile. She had lost herself watching out the window as their car service drove them the relatively short distance to Elmont, New York for the running of the Belmont Stakes. This year had been ridiculously hot for June, but luckily there had been rain last night, finally bringing temperatures down and making for a nice day for the race.

Chelsea had been excited when Alex had invited her to accompany him on the trip, promising box seats and the opportunity to mingle with some of New York's elite horse racing fans. Alex had been vague about who's box seats they would be sitting in, leaving that it was a business perk. She had learned weeks ago when not to push, and had happily gone to find a dress in her immense closet.

As their car entered Belmont Park, Chelsea craned her neck to see the sights. She had been to Louisville for the Kentucky Derby multiple times as both a young child and later as an adult. Elmont, New York was far from Louisville, yet Chelsea assumed there would be many similarities between the two venues. Since she first read *Misty of Chincoteague* as a young girl, Chelsea had loved horses way before she loved boys or rubbing elbows with the rich for that matter. As she smoothed down her polka dot dress, she realized just how happy she was to be there.

"Thank you for bringing me today Alex. I'm looking forward to our day." She leaned over to kiss him on the cheek, her genuine excitement both surprising and pleasing him.

"You're welcome. I'm glad you're here." he said simply.

Before she knew it they were seated at a table having lunch in The Belmont Room, their view from the second floor of the clubhouse quite enjoyable for any horse race fan. Walking to their table, Chelsea had been delighted to see some celebs seated here and there and spotting SJP and her husband Matthew left her with a big smile on her face.

Magically drinks appeared at their table, and Alex was quick to explain they were known as the "Belmont Jewel," a new and more refreshing twist on the traditional Belmont Breeze. She sipped it gingerly, but quickly realized it was very similar to the whiskey sours she enjoyed, although the pomegranate juice made its taste unique.

After lunch Alex had taken Chelsea for a walking tour of Belmont Park, before eventually finding their way to their box seats. She was impressed to see their seats were just above the finish line and winner's circle. They had wait service and Chelsea found herself drinking another Belmont Jewel. Holding onto her hat, she swiveled her head to get a good look at the track. As most race fans did, she knew the track for the Belmont was the longest in a horse's journey to win the Triple Crown. And after last night's rain, the dirt track promised to be sloppy.

People watching was one of Chelsea's favorite hobbies of attending any social event and today's crowd did not disappoint. Although not as over the top with their hats as Derby fans, there were plenty of well dressed men and women to sit and watch. She suddenly realized Alex was talking to someone who had sat down on the other side of him. She was astonished to see it was Victoria, the woman who had hosted the Heart Ball a while back.

It was easy to see from Alex's body language that he wasn't happy to see her. Leaning forward to be noticed, she interrupted their conversation.

"Oh hello! Victoria, right? We met at the Heart Ball." she said pleasantly enough. She was not prepared for the icy greeting Victoria shared.

"Ahh yes, Alex's dance partner. The one who somehow got locked in the bathroom."

Alex protectively put his arm around Chelsea, making his own comment in response to her remark. "Chelsea is my guest today. I didn't realize you were planning on being here."

Victoria announced airly, "Well it is my box, why would I not be here?"

Alex's eyes narrowed, but he kept his voice even. "If it's a problem we're here, we can move."

Victoria held his gaze for just a minute before answering. "Don't be silly Alex. There's plenty of room for all of us. I'm just surprised to see you bring an employee from Hudson & Butler."

Chelsea knew a dig when she heard one, and her response popped out before she took the time to decide if it was smart or just being a smart ass. "Oh Alex isn't just my boss. I'm sleeping with him too. Every girl's wet dream, am I right?" She winked at Victoria as she sipped her drink, her eyes never leaving Victoria's face. She was surprised and pleased to see Victoria's look of displeasure.

When she felt the pressure of Alex squeeze her shoulder, his arm still around her, she realized perhaps she should have left it unsaid. She quickly apologized. "Please forgive me, that was unnecessary. I think my drinks are catching up to me!"

Luckily for all of them they were suddenly distracted by the bugler calling the horses to the gate, the race soon to start. Despite the intensity of their conversation, Chelsea jumped to her feet, the sound of the bugle raising the hairs on her arms. She adored the call of the bugle and turned her full attention to the horses as they paraded to their posts.

Before they knew it, Ruler on Ice was standing in the Winner's Circle, Chelsea thrilled to have her horse pick as the winner. She had surprised both Alex and herself with how animated she had become over cheering a horse onto the finish line. Alex had let her choose a horse to bet on and she was now due a nice payout. Having witnessed the blanket of white carnations bestowed upon Ruler on Ice, she was ready to go and collect.

Alex asked her to wait, knowing the performance of "New York, New York" was about to take place as part of the after race celebration. She was thankful to see Victoria had already departed and allowed herself to join the crowd in singing her heart out to the song Frank Sinatra had made famous. She smiled at Alex, his bemused expression not lost on her.

It was a quiet ride home as Chelsea slept, her hat on the seat beside her, her head resting on Alex's shoulder. He watched her sleep, thankful to prolong the conversation that was sure to come sooner or later. Alex wasn't in a hurry to find out, but could imagine how well Chelsea was going to take finding out who Victoria really was.

He met Victoria in college and had stupidly let her manipulate him into marrying her after graduation. They had been young and impulsive, their good times only carrying them so far once their relationship was legally binding. Sooner or later her true personality emerged, her behavior often more of a temperamental spoiled brat than a young woman in love. But still, Victoria's father had bankrolled the start up costs for Hudson & Butler Publishing and Alex felt a sense of obligation to work hard to keep their marriage alive. It had worked until he realized she was counting on that, manipulating him in a variety of ways to delay the inevitable. After that he was done.

He had divorce papers ready to serve her when she had shared her mother had stage 4 breast cancer. She had been an emotional wreck and leaned into Alex for support. He knew first hand what it felt like to lose a parent you were close to and had stashed the papers somewhere in the bottom of a drawer. Eventually they had gone their separate ways, Victoria content to let the business continue to run as it always had, with Alex doing the work and Victoria rebuilding her life after losing her mother. He had learned a lot of lessons being married to a rich socialite, lessons he did not care to repeat, even with Chelsea, as crazy as he was about her.

FOURTEEN

Sitting at her desk sipping her coffee, Chelsea stared gloomily out the window. She realized she was still processing the news Alex had dumped on her last night over dinner. She had been rehashing the highs of their day before, the Belmont Stakes one of her best days ever. The only flaw had been that Alex hadn't told her who the box had actually belonged to, causing her instincts to tell her he was hiding something. She had to admit it had come as an unexpected surprise to learn Victoria was to thank for their incredible seats. Her instincts also told her Victoria did not like her, although she had no idea why. Alex's news had explained a lot.

Despite her best efforts, it had been hard to hide her shock to learn that Victoria was actually Alex's ex-wife. Her emotions had been a rollercoaster from disbelief to anger to cautious acceptance. She had so many questions, but stuck to the big one–why had Alex taken so long to tell her? He had been defensive at first, but it did not take long for him to apologize when she demanded an explanation.

Somewhere along the way she realized Alex knew her well and expected her to lose her cool over this news. She had taken a minute to count to ten and keep her response calm. They both had a past and she had to admit hers was a lot uglier than his any day of the week. She had asked some simple questions about how they met, when they were married, and how long they were married. The big one, such as why did they get divorced, she decided to keep to herself, but only for now.

Alex had solved the mystery as to why Victoria seemed to dislike her so much. It was slightly comforting to assume she was jealous of her relationship with Alex and Chelsea could hardly blame her for that. Still, she should know better than anyone that a scorned woman can be dangerous. She would make every effort to keep a low profile when it came to Victoria and definitely try her best not to make any more triggering remarks. Turning back to her desk she sighed loudly knowing that for her, it would be easier said than done.

It was just after lunch when Alex popped into her office, clearly agitated. Chelsea leaned against her desk, waiting for Alex to drop whatever he had brought into the room. She watched him pace the room like a tiger, his handsome face annoyed.

"Just spit it out Alex." Chelsea finally said. "How bad can it be?"

Alex stopped his pacing and came to stand before her, his arms crossed across his chest. "It's Victoria. She wants us to publish her book."

Chelsea's head rolled as she took in what he said. Alex had not shared a lot of details about their marriage or divorce, but after the other day, knew this could not be good news. "Victoria? You're kidding!" she asked, her tone flat.

He nodded before adding, "Since our divorce she's rarely more than a blip on how stupid and naive I was in my twenties. Before Saturday, I hadn't seen her since the Heart Ball. I was startled to see her name in my appointment book for today."

Chelsea found it hard to believe Alex had ever been naive, but then again, she had been able to work her way around him to get herself hired at Hudson & Butler months ago. It was funny how things could change over time, knowing she would have never guessed they would end up in the relationship they had today.

Seeing Chelsea's face, Alex came to stand in front of her. He leaned his hands on the desk Chelsea rested against, bringing his face close to hers. "I know you two aren't book buddies, but you are going to join me for this meeting and give me the support I need from you. Any questions?"

Returning his gaze, Chelsea smiled before answering, "Yes actually. Are you crazy? Victoria hates me! Why do you need me in on this?"

As he leaned in closer to her, she felt her skin start to warm. "Consider this the personal favor you owe me. As I recall you are very good with returning a favor. Right?"

As Alex straightened, his eyes were dark on hers, but his face was very serious. She could see he would leave her no choice. "Any other questions?" he asked, assuming they would move on.

Never one to back down, Chelsea pressed her point. "Yes, as matter of fact. Has she ever written a book before? And if she's so annoying, why don't you tell her to go jump off the Brooklyn Bridge? There are plenty of other publishers to be had in New York City."

Alex's expression was grim as he answered her. "We will be publishing her first book, because…because she's the Hudson on the door. And you and I will be handling her account together. Any other questions?"

More than taken aback to learn this news, Chelsea answered casually. "No sir." Not for now, Chelsea thought to herself. "I'll be there. At what time?" Chelsea answered tersely.

His swift kiss to her cheek and soft thank you barely soothed her jagged nerves over this newest development. As he moved to her door, he turned back to say, "My office at six o'clock." He added as an afterthought. "And be early. Please."

For the second time in twenty four hours, Alex had dropped a bomb on her. She knew him to be an upstanding guy and way better than any man she had ever been with, but still, she found all of this unsettling to say the least. She couldn't help but wonder, was there more to come? What else had Alex failed to disclose to her?

She would be the first to argue that withholding information was not the same as lying, even though if you were the one on the receiving end, they often felt the same. Even if Alex wanted her to assist with this project, she had to wonder how Victoria would feel about her working on her book too? Something told her it was not going to go over well. Pouring herself more coffee, she knew she would find out soon enough.

FIFTEEN

Chelsea sat on Alex's leather sofa, her hands in her lap, waiting nervously for Victoria to arrive and get their meeting started. She was thankful she was dressed in her favorite sheath dress, the design highlighting her assets. As she sat watching Alex fidget with papers at his desk, she realized they were matching, Alex's tie the same shade as her pink dress.

"Alex! Do you have another tie in your desk drawer?" she asked suddenly.

He looked up at her crossly. "What? Why do I need another tie?"

The door opened suddenly, the soft knock barely a courtesy. They both watched as Victoria swept into the room, her red dress showing off her own assets.

"Hello Alex! Ready for our next bestseller?" she asked as she went to stand beside his chair, her face warm and excited to see him.

As he cleared his throat, Chelsea realized Alex appeared somewhat nervous as well. "Right on time Victoria. We are interested to see what you've brought us." He responded while motioning to where Chelsea sat.

They both watched as her expression changed, Victoria not bothering to hide her annoyance to find Chelsea there. "What is she doing here?" she asked flatly.

"I asked her to be here. She is our best editor and has a way of working magic with the books she takes on. I assume you want only the best working on your book?" Alex had pushed back his chair, choosing to walk around the other side of his desk to stand between the two women.

"What I want is for YOU personally to take on my book." Victoria said in her biting tone she had no doubt perfected years ago.

Chelsea watched as Alex turned on his charm, clearly wanting to soothe her ruffled feathers. "Of course I'll be working on your book too. I can't wait to read it and then Chelsea and I will edit it together before it hits the presses."

With a loud thud, Victoria plopped her manuscript down on Alex's desk. "Fine. You will need to make copies. I want to preserve this one as it's my only original."

Alex furrowed his brow before asking, "But you do have this saved somewhere, right?"

Victoria sneered at him. "I'm not new to the publishing world Alex. I understand the nuts and bolts of using technology to get your story out into the world."

Victoria picked up her bag and headed for the door. Suddenly she paused, turning her icy stare to Chelsea. "I'm not sure if you're aware, but I'm the Hudson on the wall when you come into this building. The big gold letters make me your boss. I expect this to be your top priority until it's ready for the presses. But if you do screw it up, just know you will be out on the street." Victoria turned back to Alex, her expression warmer. "I'll be in touch. Soon!" she added. With that she was gone.

Chelsea took a deep breath and released it before getting up to go and stand before Alex. "So, still think it's a good idea for me to be on this project?"

Alex pulled her close, hugging her before he mumbled into her hair, "I wouldn't have it any other way."

He held her at arm's length, his eyes warm on hers. "I'm going to go make two copies and then we'll go home and get busy."

Chelsea cocked her head to one side, pulling him back to her, her hands on his back side, her body pressed into his. "You're the boss. I'm always happy to get busy with you." she said.

He pulled away from her with a laugh. "Save that for later. First we've got some work to do. You go order sushi and I'll be back."

Chelsea watched him walk out the door, feeling uneasy that this could not possibly work out well. Victoria might not be married to Alex anymore, but she recognized that she still wanted Alex. She couldn't help but wonder if Alex ever thought about Victoria in that way too. She would just have to make sure he didn't have the opportunity.

SIXTEEN

It was getting late and Chelsea took a minute to rub her eyes, taking a break from the pages of Victoria's book, the lines beginning to blur. She lay her head back on the pillow to watch Alex. This was her favorite way to see him, his hair unruly, his late night shadow making him appear rugged, his brown eyes big behind his glasses. His king sized bed was one of her favorite places to read, the linens lush but cozy, the warmth of him under the covers comforting. She had never realized intimacy could be much more than just having sex until she met Alex.

They had been reading for a while now and Chelsea was already over half way through the book. She was dying to talk to him about the story, but didn't want to disrupt his reading. Instead she got up and stretched before picking up their discarded sushi containers and her oversized empty chai tea latte before heading to the kitchen.

As she put things away and found a bottle of red wine to open, she had to admit the story was good. She wasn't sure what she had expected, but not that. The title, *Deathbed,* had immediately caught her attention and she had been hooked from the very first page. She was curious as to what Alex thought.

As she worked to take the cork out, she smiled as she felt Alex come up behind her, his arms encircling her at her waist. "I hope you're pouring a glass for me." he said before burying his face in her neck.

"I am. I needed to take a break. There's a lot to process in this story. What do you think?"

He went to retrieve two wine glasses, holding them out to her as she poured. "You first. What do you think?" he said as he took his first sip, the tannins reaching out to his nose first before embracing his taste buds.

"I have to say it's good. The idea of a woman who's powerful husband has taken his mistress's baby to replace the baby he and his wife lost. And then the way her mother decides to drop that bomb on their daughter when she's on her deathbed. You're losing a mother, but surprise, you have another one out there! The story has so much loss and so much deception. The betrayal is cringe worthy and heartbreaking at the same time." Chelsea paused for a moment, taking a sip of her wine. "I hate to say it, but I can relate." she added softly. "In a different way of course, but betrayal is betrayal."

Alex's eyes were intense as he listened to Chelsea. He set his wine glass down and went to her, embracing her in the warmth of his strong arms. "So do we blow our alarms off in the morning and keep reading or do we go to bed? Your call."

Chelsea was torn. It was just past midnight and less than six hours until their alarms would buzz. But still, she was wide awake and more than curious to see where Victoria's story would take them. She definitely wasn't expecting "they lived happily ever after" for the ending.

Chelsea stepped out of Alex's embrace to look him in the face. "Hmmmmm what to do? I feel like I've found a good place to stop, but I'm wide awake. And I have this half glass of wine to finish. What do you think we should do?" She cocked her head at Alex, putting the ball in his court.

"I think we go back to bed, but we reward ourselves for all our hard work after hours. The rest can wait until tomorrow."

Chelsea smiled, "You're the boss. If it's time to quit, it's time to quit. How do you suggest we reward ourselves?" she asked.

He took her free hand and led her back to the bedroom. "I have a few ideas." he said with a smile.

Alex was propped up on his pillows struggling with his conscience as it wrestled with what to do. Chelsea had long been asleep and he found himself drawn back to the book. Having finished it in the very early morning hours he found himself wondering a few things about the story. The tale of a powerful man taking what he wanted to suit his own needs was as old as time itself, but the characters in the story were disturbingly familiar.

Unexpectedly the story had taken Alex back to the time when Victoria's mother had been diagnosed with breast cancer. It had been a difficult time for Victoria and she had been devastated when her mother passed away. She had always been close to her mother as her father, a powerful business man in the community, was often busy working and missing from the dinner table.

Alex had to give Victoria credit for writing a hell of a book. He never saw it coming, assuming the title *Deathbed* was seemingly inspired by her own mother's death. The betrayal Chelsea had referred to as the mother lay on her deathbed, needing to confess the sins of her husband to their daughter with her last dying breath was jarring. The accusations of the story were heavy burdens for anyone to carry, but what kept Alex awake was the concern of whether her book was fact or fiction. Although Victoria's names were fictitious, her name on the cover could possibly garner some unwanted speculation.

After her mother's death, Victoria had become a different person. She had become a recluse, drinking heavily, refusing to go into work, relying on Alex to take care of it all. He had assumed it was her grief that had driven the change in her, but now he had to wonder if there really had been a deathbed confession from her mother. News like that would be life changing, and combined with her mother's death, a lot for her to handle. He had to wonder if Victoria had been able to write her characters so well because they had been real people for her. What troubled Alex the most was the fact that her father would surely not want to see her story in print, let alone revealing whoever the mystery mistress was.

Should he tell Chelsea his concerns about Victoria's book? He struggled even more to know what to say to Victoria. His first instinct was to discourage her from publishing the tell all tale, but he doubted Victoria would go for that. Another option would be to edit the hell out of it making it less specific and accusatory. The best choice seemed for her to publish it under a pen name. He was going to need to talk to Victoria as soon as possible. As Alex's alarm went off, he reached over to kiss Chelsea on the cheek before heading off to the shower. It was going to be a very long day, his lack of sleep the least of his worries.

SEVENTEEN

It had been just forty eight hours since Victoria had left her book with Alex and Chelsea. The book had become Chelsea's newest obsession, and she couldn't wait to edit the book and take it to market. Given her unexpected enthusiasm, Alex had made the decision to talk to Victoria alone and in private, before he brought Chelsea into the big picture. Now he stood on the doorstep of her home in Prospect Park South, the car ride to Brooklyn giving him time to think.

He was greeted with a warm smile from Victoria as she opened one of the heavy double doors to him. "Alex, thank you for coming all the way out. Let's go into the library."

Having acknowledged her with a brief, "Of course," he followed her nervously into the library. This room had always been one of his favorite rooms in the massive home. French doors opened to reveal a wall of mahogany floor to ceiling shelves built around a giant marble fireplace. The shelves were lined with books, some of them first editions or books no longer in print. The ladder hanging from the top shelf belied the possibility anyone ever read any of the books. Still, the room felt comfortable and Alex settled into one of the leather chairs that faced the large desk Victoria chose to sit behind.

"Can I get you anything to drink? Tea, coffee, Perrier?" Victoria asked, her eyes warm on his. Seeing one brow arch briefly she added, "My home is a dry space now. Took me a while to figure it out, but I learned that alcohol and I aren't good for each other. Unlike us perhaps?" She looked around the room before adding, "We had some good times in this room, didn't we Alex? It was always your favorite room in the house, wasn't it?" Her voice was soft, seemingly twinged with both regret and fondness.

Alex looked around the room appreciatively noting very little had changed since he had seen it last. "It is a beautiful room, but as I recall the last time I was here we were signing divorce papers." Seeing her face darken, he added hastily, "You're right though, we did have some good time here."

Victoria came to stand in front of him, crossing her legs dramatically and leaning in towards him. "As I recall this is the room where you proposed to me, right before you had your way with me on my father's desk."

Taken aback, Alex responded the best he could, his eyes meeting hers square on. "There was that, you're right. But that was a long time ago. We aren't those two naive kids anymore, are we Torie?" His voice was quiet, not wanting to encourage her in any way, that he was there for professional reasons only.

She searched his face intently before abruptly turning to go back to the large leather chair behind the desk. "So. You're here on business. You've read my book?"

Relieved she was moving on, he nodded as he answered her. "I have. You always wanted to be a serious writer and now you've written your first book. Congratulations."

She surprised him once again with a bitter laugh. "I don't know how much I had to do with it. I'm merely the messenger. The story wrote itself, painful as it was."

Choosing his words carefully, he asked, "So your mother did make this confession? On her deathbed?"

Her face darkened again. "You think I could make this story up, knowing I was the one to sit with my mother when she was on her deathbed, my father off taking care of business as usual?"

Not able to hide his feelings anymore, he rubbed his hand through his hair before saying anything. "Jesus! I'm so sorry you went through that. Why didn't you ever say anything?"

Her smile was brittle as she challenged him. "Would it have made a difference Alex? You had one foot out the door, remember?" Her eyes suddenly watered as she mumbled, "It was hell losing both of you at once! There were some pretty dark days. Drinking was my savior, but only for so long."

He wanted to hug her, wishing he could take it away. Her mother had always been warm and kind to him, welcoming him into their home and the family. It had hurt him to lose her, but nothing like the pain of suddenly losing his own father. He empathized with her, but knew trauma like what they had been through has to be dealt with head on, one day at a time. There were no shortcuts, only time able to eventually dull the pain.

Finally he went to her. He didn't say anything, just pulled her up out of the big chair, and pulled her to him. "It must have been hell, Torie. I'm so sorry I wasn't there for you. I tried, but I didn't know it was that bad."

She had always been so petite and he was startled by how easily she fit back here again, in his arms. He sensed her breathing him in, but her mumbled "I've missed this Alex" was the reality check he needed. Abruptly he pulled away. "I came to talk about the book. We need to talk about it Victoria."

She fell back into her chair, reeling from the rollercoaster he put her on. "What about it? What's there to say?" she asked shortly.

"Are you serious about putting this in print? Do you honestly think that's wise?" he asked.

"Isn't that the point Alex? Did you think I wrote it to sell books? I don't give two shits about being a New York Times bestseller. I want people to know what a disgusting, poor excuse of a man my father is. He deserves so much more, but a girl can only do so much."

Once again he paused, choosing his words carefully. "But is that really a good idea to expose him to the public? He's very well known and respected, and it could backfire on you, on Hudson & Butler. And what about his mistress? Your actual mother? How is she going to feel about all this, knowing you're talking about her?"

"Oh my god! I hadn't thought of that!" her tone dripped with sarcasm. "Maybe someone else will feel betrayed? Maybe someone else will have their life uprooted? I don't care! Join the club, the more the merrier!" Her voice was brittle.

Alex narrowed his eyes. "I'm serious Victoria. This book could have some consequences you can't even see coming yet."

"Fine. What do you suggest?" she asked.

"There are a few options. Chelsea and I will edit the hell out of it, making it less accusatory. Have you considered publishing under a pen name so you're protected?" He said, trying to make it seem like it wasn't a choice.

"No." She said it matter-of-factly, dismissing his choices. "Edits should be minimal and approved by me. My name will be on this book because that will sell it to the people I want to know this shocking story. In fact I've already started planning a pool party to launch the book. Of course you will need to be there."

Alex sighed, knowing it would be impossible to move this mountain. Victoria's stubbornness had never worked to his advantage when they were married, why would it now?

"Chelsea and I will get on the edits right away." Fearing her protests he quickly added, "She loved your book by the way."

Victoria looked pleased. "Fine. I'll give Chelsea a call and set up a meeting. And I will see *you* soon too Alex". He followed her to the door, his misgivings hard to shake.

EIGHTEEN

She checked her watch again, wondering where the hell Victoria could be. They had agreed to meet away from the office and Chelsea was certain she had the day and time right. Fifteen minutes in, she had called Victoria to kindly remind her of their meeting, but it had gone straight to voicemail. She would give her another fifteen minutes and then she was out. After all, she and Alex had dinner reservations tonight and nothing was going to get in the way of that. Nothing.

She had been somewhat surprised when Victoria had called, giving her just forty-eight hours to prepare her first round of edits for *Deathbed*. Chelsea could only assume Alex had put his foot down and convinced Victoria that she would be the one to handle the editing process. Of course Alex had checked Chelsea's edits behind her, adding a few of his own. It was different having him check her work, but she realized this book was different, a very personal project for him.

Pushing her glass of wine away, Chelsea left cash on the table and collected her black leather bag, stuffing the book into it. She gave an absentminded "thank you" to the server as she left hastily. She was more than frustrated she had just wasted thirty minutes of her work day. Much as she might like to be, Victoria was hardly the only client she was working with right now.

She made the short walk back to the office and headed straight for Alex's office. Still annoyed, she barely knocked before entering, but pulled up short when she saw Victoria perched on the edge of his desk, the two of them looking cozy in their conversation. Alex noticed her immediately, saying her name before Victoria turned around, her expression triumphant.

She took a deep breath, composing herself before asking in the most pleasant voice she could muster. "Victoria! I thought we had a meeting for today?"

Barely able to contain her smirk, Victoria left her perch and turned to look at her. "So did I. I've been here waiting for you." She made a pretense of checking her watch before she continued. "Luckily Alex has been entertaining me for the past thirty minutes. I must say it's not very professional of you to be so late to our meeting." She turned back to Alex before adding one last dig. "But of course you do get special privileges don't you? How could I forget?"

Chelsea looked to Alex, noting his expression was inscrutable.

"As I recall you wanted to meet away from the office and have a glass of wine."

Victoria's feigned disapproval was not lost on Chelsea. "I'm afraid that doesn't make sense. Everyone knows I'm a recovering alcoholic. And why would I want to meet away from the place that has my name on the door? You're better off to admit your mistake than make up a story. Don't you think Alex?"

Chelsea was seething, but Victoria was hardly the first bitch she had taken on in the business world. Her smile was as fake as her as she said sweetly, "I stand corrected. I had no idea you were a recovering alcoholic. So is my mother. I hope you do better at it than she does." She cocked her head to look around Victoria to make real eye contact with Alex. "I'm glad Alex was here to entertain you and again I apologize for the miscommunication. Let me know what time works for you tomorrow and I will rearrange my calendar. Just for you." While she talked she walked up to Victoria, facing her head on.

"I'm afraid tomorrow won't work for me. We can do it now." Her look was icy, daring Chelsea to argue with her.

Chelsea checked her watch before answering her. "Actually I can only give you ten minutes now. Alex and I have dinner reservations for tonight."

Victoria threw her head back and laughed, her tone patronizing. "I'm afraid ten minutes will not be the time needed for this conversation. But no worries, dinner reservations are broken all the time. It seems you'll have some free time tomorrow though dear."

Finally Alex spoke, coming around the desk to stand by Chelsea. "Actually we are going to make those reservations and if tomorrow doesn't work for your schedule, you let us know what day will work for you."

Victoria's face darkened perceptibly before she choked out her words. "I want this meeting and I want it now Alex!"

Unruffled Alex answered her smoothly. "I understand that, but you're an adult and you understand sometimes plans change. It's Chelsea's birthday and I've planned a very special night for us. She will see you tomorrow or whatever day works for you."

He handed her very expensive bag to her, walking her to the door as he talked. "Take care Victoria." And with that he closed the door behind him. Chelsea stood there somewhat stunned he had done that. As she went to speak, he motioned for her to be quiet, listening at the door. He could hear her talking to his secretary, asking for pen and paper. When they heard the elevator ding, he finally turned to Chelsea.

"What did I tell you about poking the bear?" he asked, half serious but half teasing.

She went to stand in front of him, her hands on her hips. "Me! What about her? She stood me up! Then she tried to put me in my place *after* blaming me for missing the meeting!"

Alex closed the small gap between them before putting his hands through her arms and pulling her outraged body closer to him. "I know, she's done it to me before too. She likes to play dirty and is not someone you want to cross."

Chelsea all but snorted. "Whoops! Too late for that!"

"It's not too late to play nice. After all-" he was saying before Chelsea interrupted him. "Because she's my boss?! You have to do better than that Alex!"

He moved back and took her chin in his hand, his hold firm. "I was going to say because you're the one who has me. She's all alone and has been through a lot. We can afford to cut her some slack."

Chelsea stared at him for a half minute trying to decide how she wanted to play this. Was he serious? Who hadn't been through a lot? But he did make a good point. She was the one he was sleeping with, the one he was in a relationship with and that did feel good.

"You're right. I am the lucky girl. Now how about those dinner reservations? Can you give me ten minutes to go to my office and freshen up?"

He kissed her on the lips briefly before answering. "Anything for my birthday girl. I'll finish up here and meet you."

As she walked to her office, she quickly spied a note taped to her door. She read it quickly, shaking her head at the sender's request, *"Meet me at eight am sharp in the morning and please don't be late this time. I take my coffee black."* She had to hand it to her, Victoria knew how to stick to her story. And have the last word.

Despite Victoria's early morning request, Chelsea and Alex made the most of her birthday. He surprised her with reservations at The Polo Bar, a much sought after reservation, and Chelsea was delighted. She was a fan of Ralph Lauren's fashion line, but she was even a bigger fan of horses and Alex knew it. They shared champagne in the bar area, choosing to sit at a table for two and enjoy the plush leather banquet set off by the famous tartan pillows. Sipping her champagne, she took in the dark wood and numerous horse paintings on hunter green walls. The soft lighting and gold accents made it feel glamorous in an unexpected way. The dress code was strict and Chelsea enjoyed seeing all the well dressed socialites out for the evening.

They ordered steak and the crab cake, two of Chelsea's favorites. The Polo Bar's version of a crab cake was a deliciously serious commitment topped with crispy phyllo pieces. The New York Strip was not to be left out, seared to perfection and garnished with some interesting sauces. They finished the evening with a large slice of chocolate cake topped with whipped cream. Before they finished their champagne, Alex made a toast. "To the woman I love, adore, and cannot get enough of. May all your birthday wishes come true!"

It was a cozy, quick car ride back to Alex's place, where she was surprised to find a few large, very well wrapped boxes sitting on Alex's bar waiting for her. Chelsea turned to Alex and gave him a deep, appreciative kiss. Coming up for air, Alex told her she might want to open it before either of them got too excited.

As Chelsea untied the first pink bow carefully, she had to pause to enjoy the moment. Alex took her hand and asked with concern. 'What's wrong?"

Her look was warm as she met his gaze. "It's been a long time since someone made a big deal out of my birthday. Thank you for making me feel so loved, Alex."

He gently kissed her hand he was still holding and said, "I'm sorry it's been so long, but you're most welcome. Now open the boxes!"

She laughed at him before continuing. In the first box she found a pair of cream breeches, the classic riding pants paired with a blush button up long sleeve blouse. The second box of course held tall riding boots. When he suggested she look inside the boot, Chelsea found a gift card for riding time at one of the best stables in Brooklyn.

Delighted, she grabbed Alex's face and kissed him quickly before grabbing his hand and heading for their bedroom. He laughed as she announced, "I'm going to need your opinion on how all this looks on me!"

He followed behind her with a grin, "Always happy to help."

After unzipping the dress she'd worn to dinner, he enjoyed the show of watching her shimmy into her pants, her eyes never leaving his as she buttoned the blouse before tucking it into her breeches. She held onto his arm as she stepped into her riding boots. She was impressed everything fit perfectly and went to look at herself in the full length mirror propped against one wall. She liked having his full attention and went to stand in front of him.

"Well? How do I look?" she asked him.

"Delicious." he said as he pulled her to him, his hands reaching around to embrace her cheeks in the fitted riding pants.

She smiled, loving the feel of his hands on her. "It's been a while since I had a handsome stud under me." she said, baitina him.

"Since it's your birthday, I volunteer to be under you. You can ride me all night long." he said, his voice gruff. He nibbled her neck as he said it, his breath warm and lighting her on fire.

She moved away from him and went to sit on the bed holding one foot up to him. "The boots have to come off before the pants can come off. Get to it, stud."

They were both naked in no time, the sheets pushed away as she straddled him, their bodies moving rhythmically together. As they finished, she gave a big sigh before rolling off of him, realizing she had never loved horses more.

NINETEEN

She sat behind her desk, two black coffees and the book in front of her. She was still riding high from her birthday last night, a soft smile on her face as she daydreamed while waiting for Victoria to arrive. Promptly at eight, she swept into the room, depositing her Chanel bag in one of the chairs opposite Chelsea's desk before perching on the edge of the other one. She was dressed to the nines in cream linen pants and a light pink silk blouse. Reminding her of her new riding outfit, Chelsea greeted her with a smile and a semi-friendly "good morning Victoria," before pushing one of the black coffees towards her.

She took a sip before asking, "How are you feeling this morning? I know it's early." Victoria said, her voice polite, but conveying disinterest at the same time.

"I'm great, despite not getting much sleep last night, but thanks for asking." she replied before sipping her own coffee. She watched as Victoria's expression hardened a smidge, knowing her innuendo had not been in vain.

Puzzled, Chelsea watched as Victoria leaned towards her, clearly looking for something. "That's a shame." she said.

Refusing to let her bait her, Chelsea said nothing. "No engagement ring for the birthday girl? Oh that's right, you're just sleeping with the boss. For now." she added the last bit with a smug sneer, knowing Chelsea would feel her jab.

"I'm sure I don't have to tell you what a thoughtful gift giver Alex is. After all you were married to him. Once." Now it was Chelsea with a smug smile. "He surprised me with time for horseback riding at Prospect Park Stables. And a new outfit."

She had Victoria's attention now, her one brow arched in surprise. "You know how to ride or you're taking lessons to learn how to ride?"

"It's been a while since I've been on a horse, but I've always been a good rider. Do you ride?" The curiosity went both ways.

"Of course. I always loved horses and took lessons from the time I was a young girl. I entered competitions here and there."

Chelsea paused for a moment before returning some equally personal information. "I begged my mother for lessons after I read the book *National Velvet*. I would watch the movie over and over again. Who didn't want to be Elizabeth Taylor?" She asked the question lightly.

Victoria looked at Chelsea, giving her a crisp nod. She cleared her throat. "Well, should we get on with it? You're not my only appointment this morning."

Swiftly brought back to reality, Chelsea pushed her copy of Victoria's book towards her abruptly. "Of course." She tapped the top of the book adding, "Personally I loved your book. Both Alex and I made edits which are well marked and waiting for your approval. I'm curious though what your point is with the story?"

Staring at her blankly, Victoria asked, "What do you mean? My point?"

She pushed on, Chelsea in her element as she discussed the book without bias. "You titled it *"Deathbed"* but you ramble in some places where it's hard to tell if the story is about the mother's confession on her deathbed or the father's infidelity and other atrocities he commits over the years. I mean the daughter has just learned she has another mother out there because her father gave his wife a new baby when she was devastated by the loss of their own baby. The fact that it was his mistress's baby adds so many layers to the story."

Victoria's face was stony, her tone full of rage. "Her father did the unspeakable! He took a baby from another woman and gave it to his wife like it was a Chanel handbag!"

"Yes, but did he do it out of love for his wife? Were they both not devastated at the loss of their baby girl? Did she even question it when he magically appeared with this new baby?" Chelsea loved to play devil's advocate.

Now Victoria stood up, her fists clenched. "People lose their children everyday, but no one would ever think to go and get another child. Who does that?"

Chelsea was surprised by her reaction, but continued with her line of thinking. "Well when it's done legally, it's called adoption. I want to know more about this baby swapping. Did he pay her off? Was there a missing baby report filed? If she was his mistress, one can assume her moral compass is already skewed. And he knows this little girl is already half his. And his wife is heartbroken, unable to go on. Until she holds this new baby girl and she has a reason to live again."

Chelsea had stopped talking, watching as a pale faced Victoria slowly sat back down in her chair. "I think I need some water." she said bleakly.

She was out of her chair quickly, pulling a bottle of Perrier from her small office refrigerator, handing it to Victoria, curious about her reaction. She gave her a few minutes before she spoke.

"Victoria, are you okay? Did I say something to upset you?"

She took one more sip before turning to Chelsea. "This story, this story is very personal. And. . .and you bring up some points I didn't think through. It caught me off guard."

Chelsea studied her closely, thinking about her words. Softly she asked, "When you say personal, do you mean your mother actually confessed this? On her deathbed?" She was floored to think any of this could be true.

It took her a minute to pull herself together but when she did her tone was icy. "Yes, it's my story. I assumed Alex would have told you when you were reading it together. My mother had cancer and on her deathbed, confessed this to me. I was devastated to lose my mother, but this. . .this was the unthinkable!"

She stood up before she continued. "The point of this story is for everyone to know what a monster my father is. I have no idea how it all went down and neither did my mother. But it just proves my point that he believes he's above the law, that he can justify anything he does."

Now it was Chelsea's turn to sit in her chair. Her mind was whirling with a thousand questions, but she wasn't sure how to proceed. Choosing her words carefully, she asked, "Are you sure that's the point you want to make? Isn't the real story to honor the relationship you had with your mother? And that you have another mother out there? It feels like your mother was worried about you being alone and hoped you would find her. Rich, entitled men are a dime a dozen Victoria, but not everyone has two mothers. That's the real story."

She picked up her bag and gave Chelsea one last icy look. "My mother is dead, the book will be printed as is. Find someone to design the cover and get it printed. This meeting is over."

With that she was gone, both women reeling from the emotional conversation. She could only hope she could get to Alex before Victoria did. She could imagine the earful she would give him, but she had her own bone to pick with him. Why in the hell hadn't he told her *Deathbed* was a true story?

TWENTY

It has been a week since their emotional conversation and the fallout had been swift. Of course Victoria had gotten to Alex first which had led Chelsea and Alex to have their own loud and heated conversation. He had assumed she would go over the said edits and had never imagined she would dig deeper into understanding the story. Clearly Alex had forgotten what the real editorial process was and thought Chelsea had deliberately provoked Victoria. He argued he had told her Victoria's mother had died from cancer and her conversation with Victoria had been insensitive. From here on out, Alex would handle the book although the wisdom of it being published still appeared to be up in the air.

After a long week, Chelsea was dressed in her riding outfit and headed to the riding stable, the car service taking her to Brooklyn. She had scheduled her time for riding, excited to familiarize herself with a new riding path on a beautiful horse.

As they pulled into the parking area of the stable, Chelsea was confused that the sign did not say Prospect Park Stables, but rather a different name. She leaned towards her driver Kenny to ask. "Excuse me, but I think this is the wrong stable."

He turned to smile at her, "No, I got word from the boss as I was picking you up. This is correct ma'am. Enjoy your ride."

Still not sure, Chelsea got out of the car and headed toward the stable. She was met warmly by a young girl with a clipboard. She soon discovered her name was on the list and assured her they had a beautiful horse just about ready for her.

She was delighted when she saw the trainer walking the horse towards her, his likeness to the *National Velvet* horse uncanny.

"He's beautiful!" She exclaimed when they were close enough.

The trainer smiled. "We call him Taylor. He's calm and will give you a great ride. Ready?"

As she stuck her boot in the stirrup, Chelsea was surprised she felt a bit emotional. It had been a long time since she had been on a horse, a simpler time, when the world was still warm and fuzzy for her younger self.

"I'll lead you both around the paddock a few times and then I can go with you along the riding path since it's your first time to ride here."

He led the horse around the first couple of times until Chelsea grew impatient and respectfully asked to do it herself. She picked up the pace to a trot, moving her body up and down in sync with the horse. "You look good!" the trainer yelled, encouraging her.

She pulled up to him. "I'm ready for the riding path! How many miles is it?" She asked excitedly.

"You've got three to four miles. It's well marked, but I'm happy to go with you." He said, looking at her questioningly. When she shook her head no he added, "Just remember to stay on your side and be aware of other riders."

They both turned their heads as someone announced "Don't worry about her. I'll ride with her." Seeing the trainer's look of confusion she added sweetly, "We're old friends."

He turned to Chelsea for confirmation. She stumbled over her words, more than taken aback to see Victoria there. "Um, yes we know each other."

Victoria smiled from her saddle. "Shall we ride?"

Chelsea waved her hand in front of her. "After you!"

Aware the trainer was watching them both, Victoria turned back to him before she trotted off. "No worries Hank! I'll take good care of Taylor and our new girl!"

For a while they rode single file, the path more busy close to the stable. Chelsea was relieved it didn't really encourage conversation and started to let herself relax and enjoy her ride.

They were probably a couple of miles in when the path widened as they moved through a field. Victoria slowed her horse so that Chelsea could move her horse up beside hers.

"What's wrong Chelsea? Cat got your tongue today? No points you're dying to share with me?" Victoria asked, her tone civil, but just short of friendly.

Chelsea rolled her eyes, forcing herself to sound sincere. "About that. I had no idea this was so personal to you and never would have said anything if I had known. I apologize for being insensitive. I had no business poking my nose in."

Victoria looked across to her. "Thank you for saying that Chelsea. How is my cover coming along?"

She turned her gaze from the path for a minute, her surprise evident. "Alex told me he would take care of your project. I'm not sure how the cover is going, sorry."

She could tell Victoria was processing this information, clearly news to her. "I will talk to Alex about that. You have good instincts Chelsea, I can see why he wanted you on the project. It's your job to help the author flush out the best story and you were just doing your job. No need to apologize for that."

Chelsea's head was spinning, Victoria's response news to her. "What do you say we call a truce? Should we have lunch after this and get to know each other better?" Victoria asked.

"I suppose that will work for me today." Chelsea hesitantly agreed.

"Great!" Victoria was all but beaming. "I'll race you back to the stable! Loser buys!" With that she was gone, Chelsea left to stare after her.

She moved her knees to quicken her horse's trot, but she wasn't about to break into a gallop. She wasn't worried about being the loser because in her opinion, this lunch would be Alex's to pay for. It was the least he could do after raking her over the coals on Victoria's behalf.

As she brought her horse into the barn area, she was surprised to see Victoria nowhere around. She was about to thank the trainer for his time, assuring him Taylor had been a complete gentleman and she had enjoyed a wonderful ride. He looked at her with concern and asked, "Where is Ms. Hudson?"

Chelsea looked at him with surprise. "She was ahead of me. I assumed she was back already." They both turned as they heard shouts at the back of the barn, Victoria's riderless horse coming into view.

He immediately went to the trainer who then turned to Chelsea with concern. "It seems something has happened to your friend!"

Chelsea held tight to the reins of her own horse, not sure what to think. She knew Victoria was a solid rider and knew the trail well. The trainer climbed on Victoria's horse, telling the young girl who had greeted her earlier, he would be back. Stunned, she could only watch him go.

She was handing the reins to the girl as she spied the car service coming into the parking lot. She walked to the car to let Kenny know it would be a minute. She wanted to make sure Victoria was okay before she left. She was almost to the car when Alex emerged.

"Alex! What are you doing here?" she asked, more surprised than he was.

"Me? What are you doing here? When you didn't show up for your lesson, they called me to reschedule and make sure there wasn't a mis-communication. This isn't where I signed you up for riding. You're at the wrong stables!" Alex still had that annoyed tone he had the last time they talked.

"That's what I told Kenny, but he assured me the boss told him to bring me here." Chelsea replied defensively. She opened the door and asked him, "Kenny, you said the boss told you right?"

When he didn't answer, Alex said tersely, "Did you tell her that or not?"

Kenny looked uncomfortable before answering the two of them. "Not from you Mr. Butler but from Ms. Hudson. She called me on the car phone."

Alex thanked him before shutting the door. She wasn't surprised to hear him swear under his breath, but who could blame him? What the hell was going on here. It had never occurred to Chelsea that Victoria would share the same car service, although it made sense since she was the other half of the company.

Chelsea turned as they heard a four by four come to life not that far away from them. She saw the young girl driving and put her hand up to stop her. "Did he find her?"

Alex's eyes narrowed. "Find who?" He took one look at Chelsea's face before swearing again, this time not so quietly.

Without asking he jumped into the passenger seat of the four by four, his look thunderous as the girl drove off.

It seemed like hours as Chelsea waited for them anxiously. She could imagine so many things, but nothing could prepare her for Victoria's return. She was surprised to see a slightly disheveled and very irate Victoria hop off the side by side, her eyes glaring at Chelsea.

"You bitch! You deliberately startled my horse and when he threw me, you didn't even stop to help me. I could have been seriously hurt as well as my horse! What the hell were you thinking?"

Chelsea could feel her face warming as the group of people became an audience. "You're the one who took off, challenging me to race. I took my time coming back and never saw you or your horse until he returned here."

"Without me you bitch!" Victoria was enraged at her denial, standing with her fists clenched, a rubber snake in one hand. She held it up for all to see, her voice accusatory. "You know what you did, how dare you deny it!"

Chelsea felt herself go very still inside. She walked right up to Victoria and faced her rage head on with some of her own. "I don't know what you're talking about. If your horse startled, it wasn't because of me. You need to pull yourself together–bitch!"

Chelsea turned on her heel and stomped to the car. As it pulled away, she had to wonder, what had she gotten herself into?

TWENTY-ONE

She was oblivious to the playful bubbles, but the hot water was working to sooth her savage mood. She had shed her riding outfit in an angry frenzy in the middle of her bedroom before running herself a hot bath. She had her go-to playlist for times like these on her bluetooth speaker and calm was finally starting to prevail once again. She took a deep breath and exhaled it before sinking a little deeper into her soaker tub. She was grateful for her cool gel eye mask to calm her nerves and take some of the sting from Victoria's ridiculous accusations.

She should have known something was amiss when she had ended up at a different riding stable than expected. Chelsea mentally kicked herself, appalled that warning bells hadn't gone off when Victoria had magically appeared and offered to ride with her. She was getting soft, her bitchy spidey senses not what they used to be. What was most disturbing was Victoria's mental state to pull such crap. She didn't have to think long about why she was targeting her as Alex was the obvious reason. Chelsea could hardly blame her.

Chelsea had left in a huff, afraid to even look at Alex's face. If she had thought for a minute that he believed Victoria, she would have been heartbroken, an emotion much more difficult to curb than her anger. The truth was Chelsea had been in Victoria's shoes, fighting for the man she loved, not afraid to do what it took to get what she wanted. She had just never been on this side before and it was maddening as hell.

Chelsea let the music wash over her, taking the message of the latest song to heart. While her first instinct was to fight dirty with dirty, she was reluctant to let Alex see her like that. It had taken her years to realize it wasn't her pretty side. She had been a different person since her gunshot wound and was grateful to be in a healthy relationship for the first time in her life. She respected Alex too much to take that path and she realized she finally respected herself too. She knew she had Alex to thank for that, his nurturing just what the doctor had ordered years ago.

The knock on the bathroom door made her jump out of her skin and she ripped her eye mask off as the door opened. Relief flowed through her at the sight of Alex. Despite his mood, he gave her a smile to see her in the tub.

"I knocked but you must not have heard me over your music. Busy plotting your revenge?" he asked lightly.

"You scared the crap out of me! I don't know what to do. For now I'm just trying to let it go the best I can." Her voice was somber as she looked up at Alex.

He studied her for half a minute before answering her. "Okay, I'll leave you to it. But when you're done here, I'll be waiting for you with a whiskey sour and your favorite take out."

Chelsea nodded as she sank back into the tub, comforted to know Alex was here and he was supporting her. She took another deep breath and felt her mind and body start to relax for real. It was a relief to know she wasn't in this alone, but also worrisome to wonder what it would cost her? She wasn't sure how much more she could take before her old Chelsea ways would resurface. After all, old habits die hard and she was hardly likely to be an exception to the rule, regardless of Alex's support.

It was her turn to smile at the sight of him sitting in the corner of her oversized cream sectional, his glasses on busy reading the paper. He looked up as she walked into the room, moving his paper aside and patting the couch beside him. True to his word, her whiskey sour sat on the glass coffee table in front of him. As she went to join him on the couch, he told her food should arrive anytime. She wasn't really hungry, but she thanked him anyway.

He respected the space she had put between them, but turned his body to give her his full attention. "Penny for your thoughts." he said softly.

"I don't even know where to start. I get where she's coming from, she clearly wants you back and sees me as an obstacle to her happiness." Chelsea had decided an honest conversation was the best way to move forward.

Alex grimaced. "She doesn't want me back. She figured out a long time ago that I don't make her happy. She just doesn't want me to be happy and she knows you make me happy." he picked up her hand and kissed it softly.

"But you still care a lot about her. I see it in your face." Chelsea pushed him, knowing he couldn't deny it.

"You're right. We were happy together for almost ten years. We have a history together both good and bad. She put me through some shit times and she's been through some shit times. For a long time I felt like I let her down. But I've learned the hard way sometimes people don't want to be happy, they live for the angst. But she's my past Chelsea, you're my future. I love you."

She arched an eyebrow at him, a small smile playing on her lips. "You definitely have a type don't you?"

He looked confused for a moment. "Touche'! I forget you have your own gnarly past." He was relieved to see her try to make light of the situation, knowing it was far from being over. "I'm always going to be here for you, but we're going to need to find a way to diffuse her. What she really needs is a friend."

Chelsea yanked her hand back like she'd been bitten by a snake. "You must be joking! What she needs is some really good therapy and to find something else to consume her every last thought!" Chelsea looked thoughtful. "We need to make getting the book published more important than destroying me."

Alex smiled. "Exactly. Someone in the publishing world who can befriend her and help make her book all she wants it to be. I know just the right person for the job."

Chelsea released a huge sigh before she picked up her drink and took a sip. She was thinking and didn't mind making Alex wait for her answer.

"Do you believe Victoria's story is true? Do you think her mother really did make such a confession? And if she did, why isn't she looking for her biological mother?" Chelsea stared him down, her expression serious.

He reached for her whiskey sour, taking his own sip and needing a minute to think before answering her. "Honestly, it's hard to know for sure. She's the only one who knows the truth."

Chelsea cocked her head at him. "Not true. Her father knows the truth."

He couldn't hide his surprise before he answered her. "Don't even think about it! You're not going to talk to him! Why would he tell a perfect stranger something so personal?" Alex was incredulous at her suggestion.

"You're probably right, so not me. Although I'm very good at finding out what I want to know. But what about his former son-in-law? The only other man who's ever loved his daughter, who is concerned about her well being. Does he even know about the book? Would he want to see it go to print as is?"

It was Alex's turn to release a big sigh. He leaned his head back against the sofa. "I'll think about it, but don't get your hopes up. It will be harder than you think."

TWENTY-TWO

Her feet were swinging below her bar stool as Chelsea sat at the bar at The Book Room, trying to control her anxiety. It had taken some persuading, but she had finally convinced Alex to go see Victoria's father and clue him in on the book his daughter was wanting to publish as soon as possible. They were meeting this afternoon and now Chelsea waited for his arrival, anxious to hear how their meeting had gone..

Her mind whirled with a variety of scenarios. If Victoria had made it all up, Chelsea would have to give her props for being one hell of a writer. But if her mother's deathbed confession were true, that opened up a different set of possibilities. Either way, Victoria had found the perfect opportunity to wiggle her way back into Alex's life and manipulate some time with him. Chelsea sipped her whiskey sour mentally preparing herself not to overreact to whatever Alex told her.

She watched him walk across the room to her, noting his grim expression. She had a drink waiting for him, sure he would need it. She let him talk first, curious what he had to say.

He took a sip of his drink after pulling up a bar stool beside her. "Well it seems Victoria was telling the truth although her father had no idea his wife had made a confession before she passed away. He was shaken, dismayed to know she knows, but said it explained a lot about her openly hostile attitude towards him since her mother passed away."

Chelsea could see the toll it had taken on Alex to have such a conversation with his ex-father-in-law. She could only imagine how painful it had been for both of them, although obviously for one more than the other.

"I'm sorry you both had to go through that, but it's better for us to know the truth. Especially when the truth is so hard for Victoria right now. Did he say anything about her biological mother?" Chelsea was more than just a little curious.

"He did. He said we're better off to leave well enough alone and if Victoria has questions, he's hoping she will come to him." Alex still looked grim.

It seemed the obvious thing to say, but she said it anyway. "I don't think she will believe anything he has to say."

"I know. He's not happy she's publishing this book and would appreciate us not encouraging her." Alex said, his expression serious.

"Well get in line. We would all rather not be dealing with the situation at hand, but especially Victoria. It would be a lot easier if it wasn't true." Chelsea's face mirrored his seriousness.

They both sat thinking while they nursed their drinks. Chelsea was convinced the book was the distraction Victoria needed so she would be less focused on proving how unworthy she was as girlfriend material. "We are just going to have to give her what she wants. We need a kick ass illustrator to create her cover. I assume her budget is neverending. I'm going to set up a meeting with Victoria as soon as possible."

Alex looked at her doubtfully. "What makes you think she will take a meeting with you?"

Chelsea smiled. "Easy. I'll ask your secretary to set the meeting and she will assume it's with you. It won't hurt for you to be there too, but make no mistake, I'll be the one running the meeting. I'll have our art department do some mockups for her cover and create a game plan for social media. Who knows, if we start getting down to business, she actually might not be that serious about publishing her book after all."

"That would be nice, but highly unlikely. But we can do it your way. We have to start somewhere." Alex said, his voice resigned.

She was relieved he was going to let her run with the ball. She had shared her plan with Alex, but there was more to come. Chelsea had made a decision without even realizing it. That decision had prompted her game plan and she wasn't sure how much of it he would agree to. It was easy though, she would keep Alex on a need to know basis. After all, what he didn't know couldn't hurt either of them.

TWENTY-THREE

All her ducks were lining up nicely and Chelsea felt comfortable about the meeting with Victoria just minutes away. Alex on the other hand vacillated between second guessing her to his staged confidence in her. She had organized herself at the coffee table, Alex's leather couch more comfortable. Alex sat behind his desk, his sleeves rolled up, his tie loose as the workday wound down for them. Chelsea hadn't been the least bit surprised that Victoria had set the meeting for closing time. It brought a small smile to her face to think of Victoria's expression to come when she realized it wasn't going to be one on one time with Alex after all. Unbeknownst to Alex, Chelsea had taken measures for the two women to have some one on one time.

Their eyes met at the soft knock on the door before it swung open to reveal Victoria, looking stunning in a red sheath dress, accessorized with black Milano pumps and handbag. "Hello Alex. I was happy to get your secretary's call although I have to say, I was a little surprised."

"You have Chelsea to thank for that." His hand swept in her direction as she stood to greet her.

"Hello Victoria." was all she said, letting Victoria make the first move.

Her face recovered quickly moving from surprise to annoyance to her well known icy disdain. "I thought I made myself quite clear I never want to see you again, let alone work with you."

Chelsea focused on Victoria. "You did and to be honest I felt the same way. However, you've also made it clear you want your book published and it seems that you'll have to go through me to do so."

"There are plenty of qualified people at Hudson & Butler that can help me get this book published." Her tone only fueled Chelsea to push back.

She cocked her head to one side before answering, slowly walking towards her. "So true. But I assumed for a book of this caliber and a client of your stature, you would most definitely want to work with only *the best*. Did I get that wrong?"

Victoria paused, glancing at Alex before noticing the table and Chelsea's computer and a short pile of book covers laid out. "Fine. Show me what you have but know that I won't settle for anything less than what I want."

Chelsea nodded her agreement. "Of course."

Just then Alex's secretary came in requesting his presence in the conference room to settle a conflict between two junior editors. He hesitated briefly, looking at Chelsea questioningly before she waved him on. Neither of them heard him as he muttered, "I'll be right back."

Chelsea went back to the leather couch, settling back in front of her computer, her presentation locked and loaded. She patted the place next to her, clearly inviting Victoria to join her.

"If you don't mind, I think I'll sit in the chair." she said with disdain as she dragged it closer to the coffee table.

Pretending to be embarrassed, Chelsea gave a short little laugh. "I see your point. Alex may have been known to use this couch for both business and pleasure."

"I wouldn't know. When you're married to the boss, you don't have to settle for being the office slut." Victoria said.

Chelsea let it roll off her, the dig playing beautifully into her plan. She leaned toward Victoria in earnest. "I feel like we got off on the wrong foot Victoria. I'm well aware that you and Alex have a history together and I'm sure you're aware that he still cares very much for you. What he and I share is nothing compared to what the two of you have shared over the years."

Seeing Victoria visibly unclench somewhat, Chelsea pressed on. "You should know I'm passionate about what I do for authors and I want to help you make this book all you want it to be. As I said before, I regret my insensitivity during our first conversation regarding *Deathbed*. I was unaware this was your personal story you brought to life. It's none of my business how you handle the cards life has dealt you. I hope you'll accept my sincere apology, but it is my job to help authors flush out the best version of their story and that's all I was trying to do for you."

She could see Victoria thinking over what she said, trying to choose her own lane to travel in this professionally inflicted relationship. She chose to maintain her icy disdain. "I hardly need you to tell me about my relationship with Alex. However, I do want this book to be the best version of itself and I'm curious how your ideas could possibly be so earth shattering as to constitute our need to work together."

Chelsea nodded. "Of course. Let's get to it. Everything I'm sharing with you I've put into a google doc and emailed you for perusal at your convenience. There are edits you will need to approve, all of them made purely to enhance the book. I've taken the liberty of doing some cover mock ups and we are ready to bring on any illustrator of your choosing once you know how you want the cover to look. But the bigger task will be promoting the book and making sales."

Victoria waved a dismissive hand. "I've already created an event, a pool party at my home, this weekend in fact. The sole purpose of the party will be to introduce the book and encourage presales. I suppose you will need to be there. And Alex of course."

"Alex did mention your pool party and we both plan to be there." She leaned forward to make sure Victoria was listening. "But I like to create events that not only sell books, but also create a connection between the book and your targeted audience. Something that will commit your reader before they even turn the first page."

Victoria couldn't hide her curiosity. "Like what?"

"As I see it, there are two ways to go. The first and more obvious option is to create an event that not only promotes *Deathbed*, but serves as a fundraiser for the Susan G. Komen Foundation. They are the obvious choice for funding breast cancer research as well as supporting women who are struggling to survive the disease. Proceeds from the sale of each book would go towards Susan G. Komen as well as create awareness and support for the foundation." Chelsea paused to let it all sink in. "We could make it an annual event, a pretty in pink party, obviously in memory of your mother." She added the last part softly, wanting to be respectful of Victoria's loss.

She could see she most definitely had Victoria's attention. "I actually love that idea. Besides selling books, what's in it for you?"

Chelsea was startled by her question, but quickly recovered. "I don't need something to be in it for me. This is what I do, what I love to do. Help authors sell their books and share their stories."

Not able to hide her surprise, Victoria quickly moved on. "What's your other idea?" she asked.

Chelsea took a deep breath before she pressed on. "As part of the fundraiser we could bring in a genealogy specialist. Let people sign up to discover their own family pasts in exchange for a donation. After all, the story is about the truth of who you are. The big question is, do you want to sell it as fiction or autobiographical? It's easy to go either way. The choice will be yours."

It was at that moment Alex strode back into the room, his voice abrupt as he asked, "How's it going here?" Both women jumped at the sound of his voice.

Victoria stood quickly before answering him. "Chelsea has given me a lot to think about. I'll be in touch." Her last statement she directed at Chelsea, her look unreadable as she left.

Chelsea turned to Alex in triumph, not expecting to see his look of annoyance. "What have I said about poking the bear?" he asked crossly.

"Are you kidding? Did you hear her? She'll be in touch. I'm in!" Her voice was full of satisfaction, dismissing his annoyance.

"Yes I heard it all. You're playing with fire and it can come back to bite you in the ass. Have you not learned anything yet?" His voice was incredulous.

Chelsea paused, trying to sort out what he was saying. He clarified for her. "Yes, I heard it all. I know when I'm being handled and you are not the first woman to try and do so. I sent my secretary home and stood listening at the door."

Realizing he had seen through her secretary in crisis ruse, she mumbled apologetically. "So you heard all of that? Well sorry, but we needed to talk, woman to woman."

He gave a sigh before moving towards her. "I get it. And honestly you were saying all the right things. Right up to having a genealogist at the fundraiser. Too far and you know it."

Chelsea did not appreciate his tone with her and crossed her arms across her chest, her tone defiant. "I'm only saying what she needs to hear. She *IS* going to have to decide how she wants to sell this book. It will be easy to sell as fiction, inspired by her need to distract herself from her mother's death. The bigger way to sell more books *AND* raise more money for Susan G. Komen would be to sell it as the famous Hudson family autobiography. She's going to have to make a choice!"

Alex realized she was right and nodded his agreement. "You're right. The ball's in her court and we will have to wait and see how she decides to go."

He pulled Chelsea to him, holding her close. "I'm sorry I snapped. You were amazing today and if Victoria's smart, she'll let you work your magic and make her a bestseller."

She tipped her head back to laugh. "You think I have magic? What else do you think about me Mr. Butler?" her look was playful and Alex could not resist.

"I think you are by far the sexiest woman I've ever known and I need to get you home asap!" His hands traveled down the back half of her dress.

"You forgot to include the office slut. I have to admit, I do enjoy the perks though." Her eyes were dancing, hardly offended by Victoria's dig.

Alex growled in her ear. "You are way more than that and you know it. Take that back!"

She moved one of her hands from around his neck to his crotch. She looked up into his face, his eyes glowing at her. "Fine. I'm not a slut, but I do like to play dirty, especially when it's at the office."

"What did you have in mind?" he asked, his voice husky.

Chelsea went to lock his door, untying her wrap around dress as she went, pulling it down before it fell to her ankles. She went back to him, pressing her near nakedness to him. "You're the boss, Mr. Butler. I'm here to do whatever you need."

He groaned in anticipation as he picked her up and carried her to his couch. He had to admit, it was a great way to end another long day.

TWENTY-FOUR

Victoria sat at her desk in the library, the manilla envelope still unopened. Thanks to Chelsea, she was starting to realize writing this book had been only the beginning of a new chapter in her life. The last chapter had hit her hard, leaving her at rock bottom, with only her own self-preservation to help her climb out of the deep, dark hole she had found herself in. She didn't know if she could survive another such devastating chapter.

She had known writing the book would give her a reason to be in close proximity to Alex again, something she had been craving for months now. But she hadn't realized she would be competing with Chelsea for his attention. From the moment she had seen them together at the Heart Ball, she had known Alex was smitten. Victoria hated to admit it, but she could see why as she was smart, creative, and beautiful.

What annoyed Victoria the most though was Chelsea's savviness, her direct approach to speak up, and her innate ability to hit the nail on the head. She knew a competitor when she saw one and she knew Chelsea played only to win. She had to admit she had forgotten all the steps it takes to get a book in print until her initial conversation with Chelsea. She had always been happy to let Alex handle the business, but now seemed like maybe it was time for a change.

Chelsea had brought up a seemingly simple question, but the reality of it haunted her every waking thought now. How was she going to market her book? Did she really have the guts to put her name on it?

Should she use a pen name? She still hated her father and wanted nothing more than to destroy him, but now she wasn't so sure she wanted to air her family's dirty laundry. It would be easier to let the story go to market as pure fiction even if it were painfully true.

When her mother had told her she had another mother out there, she had been overwhelmed with a barrage of emotions. The hardest part had been that when she reached the anger stage, her mother was gone and that left only her father to bear her rage. Although her father would never win any father of the year awards, it had been devastating to essentially lose both her parents in one fell swoop.

It had never occurred to her to pursue finding her biological mother until Chelsea had innocently brought it to her attention. Genealogy was big business as numerous families were unwittingly discovering hidden skeletons in their closets through simple DNA tests. Loath to pursue anything so commercial, Victoria hired a PI to find out what she needed to know, the envelope in her hand, holding the answers. She was thankful there was no liquor in the house as she would have been hard pressed to resist a shot of tequila for courage.

She took a deep breath and with trembling hands opened the envelope. She wasn't sure how she felt to realize that the woman's address was right here in Brooklyn. She supposed that wasn't surprising, but it made her wonder if she had possibly ever come in contact with her biological mother, the two of them strangers, oblivious to the fact that that their DNA tied them together.

The reality check came when she saw her own birth date in the report, bringing her to an abrupt halt. This wasn't some stranger, but someone who had carried her for nine months and then painfully pushed her out of a small opening only to give her away two weeks later. Angrily she shoved the report back into the envelope and shoved it into a bottom drawer of her desk. She did not want to read anymore.

She jumped as her housekeeper knocked on the door, handing her another manilla envelope, her name scrawled across the top of it with her address.

"A courier just delivered this Ms. Hudson." Victoria thanked her, waiting to open it until her housekeeper closed the door, retreating back to her chores.

Cautiously she shook out the contents, surprised to see a collection of glossy photos fall on top of her desk. As she flipped them over, she felt herself filled with rage to see Alex and Chelsea. Some were innocent enough, taken on the streets of Manhattan while others were taken in Alex's office, the two of them caught in compromising positions.

Someone was clearly rubbing her nose in their relationship, mocking her attempts to reinsert herself into Alex's life. She felt a renewed need to put Chelsea in her place. She would show her who Alex would choose when push came to shove. Her lip curled into a sneer as she realized it would literally be a push. Or a shove, however her party guests would choose to see it.

TWENTY-FIVE

It was a perfect summer day for a pool party. The weather was warm, but the humidity was not stifling, and there wasn't a cloud in the sky. Alex and Chelsea were in the car on their way to Brooklyn. Neither of them had heard from Victoria since their meeting earlier in the week and they agreed they weren't sure if it was a good sign or not. Either way, they were committed to attending her pool party and they both sat lost in their own thoughts as the car rolled over the bridge into Brooklyn.

Just south of Prospect Park was the well known upscale Flatbush neighborhood, the large homes beautiful, the tree lined streets exuding luxury. As a well established neighborhood, many of the homes dated back to the turn of the twentieth century, including the well known Japanese House just a few streets over from Victoria's family home. Chelsea couldn't help but be reminded of her own neighborhood just south of Brush Creek and the Kansas City Plaza.

They entered the house freely, Alex showing her into the library to leave her oversized bag. Chelsea never went anywhere unprepared, particularly when she was dressed in a two piece with a crocheted silk cover-up. Pulling her Ray Bans down over her eyes, she smiled at Alex as he took her hand, squeezing it reassuringly.

"It's a gorgeous day! Let's do this!" she said to him.

She wasn't surprised to see Victoria's family home was stunning. The artwork was exquisite, but the furniture was comfy and welcoming. As they walked out double french doors to the patio, Chelsea took a moment to pause and take in the beauty of the landscaping, the pool the centerpiece of it all.

Alex looked at her questioningly. "Are you okay?"

She nodded, breathing out, "It's so beautiful." She realized she missed being in an actual home with green space, the concrete jungle of New York unable to even begin to compare.

He was still holding her hand and now raised it to his lips before leaning toward her to murmur into her ear, "Not as beautiful as you."

They were greeted immediately, a glass of champagne handed to each of them before someone who knew Alex whisked him away. Chelsea was happy to wander through the throng of guests, taking in the people and the grounds. She realized she was being watched and turned to see a pair of women watching her and clearly talking about her.

Although seemingly in their late thirties, their animated faces were child-like as they approached her. They were both dressed in colorful floral mumus with big floppy hats. Their mumus flowed around them as they gestured towards her, talking excitedly as they walked up to her.

"Well hello there!" the first one said, clearly a sister to the other.

"You're new here! And very beautiful!" the second one added.

Chelsea smiled, wanting to be friendly but not wanting to encourage a long drawn out conversation. "Hello." she said.

"We saw you come in with Alex!" said the first one knowingly.

"And that sweet kiss he bestowed on you. I bet he's your boyfriend!" said the second one, snickering softly as she said it.

"Darling sister of course she is! Just look at her! Alex would be crazy to pass her up! Ooooh I bet Victoria does *not* like you!" announced the first one gleefully.

Chelsea found herself frowning, not sure where they were going with this. "I'm sorry?"

One of them took her arm, leading her away from the server trying to move past them. "Oh don't be sorry dear! It's no skin off our noses. We don't like Victoria either!"

The second nodded sagely. "Not for years now. She's such a bitch and too heinous to ever bother to hide it!" In unison they cocked their heads looking her up and down.

"Your crocheted cover up is exquisite! Is that silk?" One of them took her hand to carefully spin her around.

"Let's see what you've got dear! Oh yes! Very nice packaging!" Chelsea was thankful her white two piece was only modestly revealing as they looked her over. She wasn't even sure what to say to them.

"Darling sister! Where are our manners!" said the first sister.

The second one looked startled and a bit mortified before extending her hand. "Oh dear! Our sincere apologies! I'm Melanie and this is my sister Ashley. We're Victoria's neighbor."

Chelsea turned to look as they pointed in the direction of a gorgeous large Victorian house that backed up to Victoria's. She watched as they both waved in unison, seemingly directed at someone in particular.

Seeing her confusion, Melanie clarified for her. "Mother's watching. She does love a good pool party. But to be fair, she's always watching."

The second sister gave her sister a small shove. "Mel, she doesn't need to know all that!" She turned back to Chelsea before asking, "And what's your name dear?"

Mel sniffed before correcting her. "She does need to know if we don't want her to think we're crazy!"

Ashley pulled up short, her eyes narrowed. "Melanie! You know what Mother has told us about using *that* word!"

They both looked at her expectantly. "Can you please forgive our poor manners dear?" asked Mel.

Ashley snatched up two glasses of champagne from the passing server. As they raised their glasses, Chelsea felt compelled to join them in their toast. "Cheers to a lovely pool party!" one sister said before taking a hefty sip from her tall flute.

"Oh yes! And to making new friends!" Said the other with a high pitched laugh. "Oh my! We still don't know your name dear!"

Chelsea hesitated before answering, "It's Chelsea, nice to meet you." she added lamely.

Suddenly Victoria appeared with a microphone in her hand, requesting her guests to come and gather around her. The sisters clapped with glee before one of them grabbed Chelsea's hand to move her along with them and do as Victoria requested.

"Alex, can you please come up and join me?" Victoria asked sweetly.

Heads turned as the crowd watched him comply, his expression impossible to read behind his aviators. He nodded at Victoria, clearly unprepared for her to link her arm through his and pull him close to her.

Chelsea could see him searching for her in the crowd and realized she might be lost standing so close to the tall flamboyant sisters in their hats.

Victoria waved her arm airly to include everyone out in the crowd. "My dearest friends! Thank you for joining me today. It is with great pleasure and a smidge of apprehension that I announce to you all the release of my first book titled *Deathbed*."

Chelsea turned to look at the sisters as they gasped together. Victoria had paused dramatically, letting her guests take in her announcement before she continued.

"As you all know," she paused again, her face full of sadness, "my dear mother passed away just over a year ago from breast cancer. It was a devastating loss and a dark time for me as I searched for ways to fill her void. An unexpected event led me to start writing and before I knew it, I had written a book. It's been a heartfelt endeavor, the fiction of it all distracting me from my pain. As you know, Alex and I make publishing books our business and Alex has been my number one supporter as I move forward with getting my book in print. I owe this masterpiece all to him. Thank you Alex!" With that she leaned over and kissed him on the cheek.

Chelsea continued to watch the sisters as Victoria talked, their reactions matching the drama Victoria was dishing out. They had crossed themselves when she mentioned her mother's death before murmuring "may she rest in peace."

When Victoria spoke of searching for ways to fill her void, Melanie had snickered before murmuring to Ashley, "Tequila can only get one so far dear!" Ashley had shushed her with her elbow and a look. Chelsea noticed another knowing look they exchanged with each other as Victoria glossed over her unexpected event. Suddenly they had turned their attention to her, demanding "are you going to let her get away with that? Isn't Alex with you now?"

Chelsea glanced up just in time to see Victoria finish the kiss she had just bestowed upon Alex's cheek.

She was quick to dismiss the kiss. "They're just friends now." Seeing their look of doubt, she pressed on with her own agenda. "I'm more curious about what event triggered her to write the story. Do you two know?"

Suddenly the two sisters were hurrying off with a "Tata dear!"

Chelsea turned to see Victoria headed in her direction. She wondered if the sisters were afraid of Victoria or if Victoria had realized they could be gossiping about her.

"Hello Victoria. It's a lovely day for your pool party." She kept her voice even, trying to not poke the bear as Alex liked to say.

"Chelsea! So good of you to join us today." Her voice was loud as she looked around to see who might be close by.

"Of course. Congrats on your announcement." she said.

Victoria was moving up close to her, taking her hands in hers. "Please don't be mad that I didn't include you in my announcement. I wasn't sure if you were here or not."

Holding her hands in the way that she was, Chelsea could feel Victoria's anger towards her. She had a look on her face that belied the words coming out of her mouth. Uncertainly she mumbled "No problem."

Raising her voice, Victoria continued talking. "Chelsea please! I didn't mean anything kissing him on the cheek! You don't need to be jealous!"

Chelsea looked confused momentarily until suddenly Victoria squeezed her wrist for all she was worth. As she tried to yank herself from her, Victoria was suddenly pulling them both into the pool yelling, "Chelsea NO!"

They went into the water with a splash, both of them going under. Chelsea came to the top first, sputtering in both shock and outrage. She looked around her for Victoria only to find her nowhere to be seen. Suddenly she saw Alex kicking off his loafers and diving deep into the pool. When he didn't come back up beside her, she realized she was not the one he had jumped in to save.

As people gathered by the pool, she swam to the side to get herself out. She thanked one of the sisters as she handed Chelsea a towel. Everyone started cheering as Alex surfaced, holding Victoria under his arm. He pulled her to the stairs and then carried her out of the pool, her body limp. People rushed over to gawk, asking if they could help.

The sisters helped Chelsea to her feet. "We knew she didn't like you! She's such a bitch! And too heinous to bother to hide it!" Chelsea turned on her heel and headed into the house. She was half hoping she would hear Alex calling out to her, but she knew he had his hands full. She could imagine the story Victoria would be telling him.

She walked into the library to retrieve her bag and get out of her wet clothes. She locked the door behind her, before carefully taking off her long crocheted dress. She couldn't care less where she left puddles as she threw her bag on Victoria's desk to retrieve a dry dress. "I'm going to kill her! She is a crazy bitch and I am done with her!"

After toweling off, she pulled the dry dress down over her head and then released her top before shimmying out of her bottoms. She plopped them down angrily on the desk before she gathered her dress and gently wrung it out over the hardwood floors of Victoria's library.

She did the same with her two piece, laying the towel out to wrap them all up securely, before she shoved the towel into her bag. She was just about to turn and go when something on the desk caught her eye.

She stared dumbfounded at the glossy photos laying on top of a manilla envelope. She didn't hesitate before shoving them into the envelope and then into her bag. Heading for the front door, she knew it was time to go and she was not about to wait around for Alex to find her. She wondered angrily how long it would take for him to check on her, before realizing she probably didn't want to know after all. As she slammed the car door shut, she knew Victoria had most definitely won this round. She took a deep breath as the car pulled away, realizing the gloves were off, revenge her favorite game to play and she would be back. The bitch could count on it!

TWENTY-SIX

She sat in the corner of her oversized couch, sipping her chai tea, and trying to calm herself down. She had been back long enough to shower and rinse out the chlorine from her dress and suit. She wasn't sure if the dress would recover, but as the minutes ticked by, she realized she was the bigger casualty of Victoria pulling her into the pool. She jumped when there was a soft knock on the door. She sat silently, hoping he would go away.

"I know you're in there Chelsea. Open the door or I will." Alex was firm, his voice deadly calm. She was still sitting there when he used his key to enter. He stopped up short upon seeing her.

"I have nothing to say to you Alex." she said, her voice abrupt.

"Perfect, because I have some things to say to you." He ran his hand through his hair, seeming to search her floor for where to start.

He took a deep breath before asking her, "First, are you okay Chelsea?"

She was incredulous. "No I'm not okay! How would I be? Your ex pulled me into her pool! And then we all got to watch you heroically save *her*! How could I possibly be OKAY Alex?!"

She realized her voice was rising until she was practically yelling. She was livid and she wasn't going to candy coat it for him.

"I know. I don't deny she deliberately provoked you by leaving you out and then kissing me in front of everyone. I get why you were mad and pushed her into the pool."

She was off the couch like a grenade had been lit under her. "What did you just say to me? You think I pushed her?" her voice was deadly quiet and yet conveyed her rage at his accusation.

She had his attention and he was smart enough to pause and rethink his word choice. "She said you were mad at her and when she tried to apologize, you pushed her into the pool. She tried to grab your hand to catch herself and you both ended up going in." He ducked just in time as she picked up her heavy crystal candy dish and hurled it at him.

"I couldn't care less about her little speech she made including her kiss because I TRUST you and know she's full of SHIT! Do you honestly believe I would PUSH her into her own pool? My god Alex! How can you think that?!" she asked heatedly.

"I believed her because you weren't there. You climbed out of the pool and just left! Besides, she would never deliberately go into the pool and everyone knows it!" Now he was becoming heated with his own words.

"And why is that Alex? Don't tell me she was worried about ruining her designer cover up she was wearing!"

It was his turn to look incredulous. "She CAN'T SWIM Chelsea! Why do you think I jumped in to pull her out?"

He suddenly realized she had assumed he had betrayed her. His expression softened and he cautiously moved closer to her. "I knew she couldn't swim. I wasn't choosing her over you, I was just saving her from drowning."

She turned away from him, being damned if he was going to see her cry over that bitch and her evil shenanigans. "I think you should go." she said, her voice husky with emotion. She turned back to him expecting him to protest. Instead she found him standing at her coffee table, looking at the photos on the manilla envelope, his face grim.

"She needs help, Alex. First the pool and now these photos! I found them on her desk when I was getting out of my wet things. Clearly she's been stalking us!"

She watched him flip through them angrily. "She was looking for these so she could show me. She said you had someone take them for you. She said you had them delivered by courier a few days ago. Why? Why would you send these to her?"

Suddenly Chelsea felt her stomach flip. He was falling for Victoria's bullshit, choosing to believe his ex-wife over her. Her voice was deadly quiet. "Listen carefully. Victoria pulled me in with her, deliberately falling in. She KNEW you would save her Alex. I didn't send these photos to her either. WHY would I? She's manipulating you Alex. She's forcing you to choose between us. Think about it carefully. Choose wisely."

He didn't say a word as he dropped the pictures on her coffee table and turned and left. Just like that, he was gone.

TWENTY-SEVEN

She was grateful the summer days were long and she had at least an hour of daylight left for one massive run. She had been numb when he left, doing the only thing she knew to do, put on her big girl shorts and select her playlist for a long run through Central Park. She loved all the different entrances along the Upper West Side, making it easy to access the park from her apartment. She was thankful for the loud music in her ears and all the people she was forced to focus on as she maneuvered around them on a busy Sunday evening.

Realizing how hard she was pushing herself, she finally stopped for a water break and to catch her breath. She was just off Fifth Avenue, one of her favorite spots as you could enter the Central Park Zoo nearby. She loved to people watch, finding it quite entertaining to watch how some of the children could work their parents over. On her very best days, she would fantasize about what her and Alex's children might look like and on her worst days, she wondered what ever possessed people to have kids at all.

She frowned as she noticed a woman sitting on a bench eating ice cream not that far away from her. As the woman looked in her direction, she was startled to realize the woman looked very much like Victoria. She was dressed casually in shorts and a t-shirt, her hair pulled back in a ponytail, the look a far cry from Victoria's designer clothes she sported everywhere she went.

Chelsea watched her curiously, her likeness to Victoria uncanny. It wasn't just her facial features, but even her movements and body language. She may be dressed down, but her demeanor definitely reminded her of a certain someone. When the woman looked her way again, Chelsea bent down pretending to tie her shoe. As she peered up, she realized she could quite possibly be looking at Victoria's sister.

As the woman walked over to throw her trash away, Chelsea got a closer look. Her mind was racing as she made the decision to follow her, hoping she would learn something about her. They had only gone a couple of blocks when the woman turned to go down into the subway. She wasn't crazy enough to get on the train with her, but maybe she could see where she was going.

As Chelsea stood amidst the throng of people, she realized she had never been on the train in her life. She mentally chastised herself as she watched the herd swarm forward to enter, each of them jockeying for a seat and to beat the doors that closed mercilessly on their own accord. She suddenly realized how isolated she was as the train pulled away, taking all the people with it. She quickly turned to head back up the stairs.

She never saw him until he was right in front of her, his face covered with his black hood. "Give me your money! Your phone! Your headphones too!"

"I don't have any money." she said defiantly.

"Yeah right! You just jumped the turnstile to get down here? Let's go bitch!" He said, looking around nervously.

"Something like that. I don't have my phone, but take these! They're Skullcandy's." She was trying to sound tough but cooperative.

He glared at her. "You stupid bitch! You're not even worth my time!" He took the headphone's she held out to him and then he struck her in the face hard enough to knock her to the ground. She laid on the concrete afraid to move, thankful to hear his feet running away.

"Hey! Hey, are you okay? You want me to call the cops?" She looked up to see an older woman, her hand reaching out to help her up, her face full of concern.

Gratefully Chelsea took her hand, sitting up cautiously, afraid to look around. "Thank you, but I'm okay. No cops." Her voice was shaky, giving her away.

The woman looked at her kindly. "A pretty thing dressed like that, you got lucky honey that shiner is all he did to you."

Chelsea nodded and thanked her again before heading back up to street level. She was relieved to see the hustle and bustle of New York that she loved, quickly blending in with the crowd as she walked the three or four blocks back to her apartment. She ran a five mile radius around her apartment any given day of the week and knew her way even as dusk was setting.

With shaky hands she pulled her key from her shorts pocket and tried to unlock her door. She jumped out of her skin as the door unexpectedly swung open to her. With relief she realized it was Alex.

"Where the hell have you been? I" he stopped abruptly as he took in the sight of her face. "Oh my god, what happened to you? Who did this to you?" He had his arm around her, bringing her to the kitchen bar and getting her an ice pack for her face.

"I went for a run in Central Park after...after you left me. I had to do something." she was mumbling to him.

He went to the couch and took one of the blankets from the basket at the end of it. He gently wrapped it around her before pulling her towards him.

"I should never have left. Chelsea I'm sorry I left you. I was just, I just needed to clear my own mind too." Holding her he realized she was shaking. He released her to go and pour her a small shot of bourbon.

"Drink this, it will help calm your nerves." he said reassuringly. He checked under her ice pack, his face grim as he assessed the damage. "Are you hurt anywhere else?"

As her eyes started to fill with tears, his grim look went to one of concern. "Where, where else are you hurt?"

She took his hand and laid it on her chest, over her heart. "Here Alex. My heart hurts way more than my face. You left me! How could you? I said choose wisely and you left!"

Her voice was small and fragile and yet he could hear her hurt and anger. He was beside himself with regret.

He pulled her to him, holding her close. "I was stupid! I'm sorry baby! I'm never leaving you again!"

She pulled away from him to go and lay the ice pack on the bar. She walked over to her couch, the blanket trailing behind her. She sat down and leaned her head against the back of her couch, closing her eyes.

Alex stared at her, not sure what to do. "When was the last time you ate Chelsea?" was all he could think to say.

She answered him, her voice quiet. "This morning. But I'm not hungry." Alex ignored her dismissive attitude.

"You need to eat something. I'll get us burgers from P.J. Clarke's." When she didn't respond he added, " You love their burgers." He didn't waste any time making the call. Then he went to run a hot bath for her, anxious to do what he could to take care of her.

"Why don't you soak in the tub while I run to P.J.'s. It will do you good." He was standing before her, both of them hearing the water running. She opened her eyes to stare at him solemnly.

She let him help her up, but still had nothing to say. He hesitated as he closed the door with, "I'll be back soon." He gave her her privacy to undress and get in the tub, the bubbles inviting, the hot water soothing. As she lay back in the water she had to admit he was right. The water did feel good and P.J.'s burgers always hit the spot. She knew she should feel grateful, but all she could feel was sadness.

TWENTY-EIGHT

The car sped along the highway, having traveled the Long Island Expressway and now almost to the rental house in The Hamptons. After their burgers last night, Alex had talked Chelsea into taking a few days off to heal her face. The Hamptons seemed like an obvious choice, just two hours from Manhattan. She had protested at first, but soon tired of it and he took her silence as a go ahead and booked a house on the water.

She had packed lightly, leaving her designer dresses at home and relying on her loungewear and suits to get her through this short impromptu vacation. She realized she had never been out of the city with Alex before and slowly started to look forward to some time away. She had packed her work bag too with some manuscripts, including the latest from her friend Kat. They had a meeting scheduled in a couple of weeks and she looked forward to her visit. She had also packed her laptop. Not only did she have some work to do, she had some research to do too.

As they pulled into the driveway of the house, Chelsea took in the property. She followed Alex to the front door letting him carry both their bags. After unlocking the door he opened it for her, moving aside so she could be first to go in. She was delighted by the house, the view of the ocean her first impression, quickly followed by a luxurious coziness she had not expected. The decor was all blue and white, the furnishings welcoming. Chelsea immediately moved to the french doors opening out to a large deck, adirondack chairs strategically placed to enjoy the view as well as a fire pit with a massive wood pile nearby.

She took a deep breath, embracing the view and the breeze coming off the water. Alex came to stand beside her, still respecting her space she seemed to need. She turned to him with a small smile. "Thank you for bringing me here Alex. I'm looking forward to some down time here."

He resisted his urge to pull her to him and instead said with a smile. "With views like these, who can resist? They're almost enough to make you forget what an ass I was yesterday." he said lightly.

Immediately her guard came back up, but she maintained her smile and merely said, "Almost. I'm going to go unpack."

Alex kicked himself for pushing. He had slept on the couch last night and he wasn't sure where he would be sleeping tonight.

"Of course. I can run to the market and get some groceries."

She nodded at him and walked back in to pick up her bag. She hesitated briefly before choosing the largest bedroom with the ocean view. It took very little time for her to put her things away before changing into some white shorts and a light pink t-shirt. She put on her oversized hat and sunglasses and eventually found a large beach towel. She went to sit out on the deck, happy to embrace the sunshine and her view.

Sitting there it was easy to be swayed into forgetting the past twenty-four hours. She decided she would give herself some time off from it all and enjoy the rest of the day. There would be plenty of time to deal with it all later. She was thankful Alex had brought her here knowing it would have been hard to just sit at home and even more impossible to show up at the office with her black eye. She wasn't sure what to do about any of it, but for today it didn't matter.

She jumped as she heard the front door slam, going to see if Alex needed assistance getting groceries in. "Need some help?" she asked.

"I managed to get it all in one trip, but thanks. Come see what treasures I found at the market." His smile was casual, but inviting.

Chelsea perched herself on a barstool, watching as he unpacked the sacks, a variety of groceries sprawled across the massive bar. She knew what a good cook Alex could be and looked on with anticipation as to what he would cook for dinner. He had lobster, rolls, kettle chips, fresh fruit and greek yogurt, steaks, salad, and new potatoes. He had pulled out some wine too, but finished with a flourish, producing a fresh baked key lime pie. Chelsea's smile grew and she reached for it demanding a fork at the same time. He was happy to oblige her, reaching across the bar as she generously handed a bite out to him.

Alex put everything away as Chelsea enjoyed her large slice of the pie. Holding out a water bottle, he asked if she wanted to go for a walk on the beach. She nodded a yes before answering. "I would love to."

He was caught off guard by her cheerful response, but quickly recovered. Holding his hand out to her, he said, "Let's go!"

She declined to take his hand, but quickly fell into step with him as they made their way to the beach.

"I've never been to the Hamptons before." Chelsea said, offering to start a conversation.

Alex looked at her and nodded. "Neither have I."

Chelsea laughed. "A first for both of us. It's different from the beaches on the Emerald Coast. Not as pretty, but ocean waves are hard to beat wherever you are."

"Where have you been on the Emerald Coast?" he asked casually.

"We had a run of summers where we would go to Destin. We would fly in and live on the beach for a week. Those are some of my happiest memories. It always seemed like being away from home gave my parents permission to let go of their usual labels and the responsibilities that went with their day-to-day routines. They would actually let themselves be happy for a while." Chelsea's voice was wistful, her memories bittersweet.

Alex listened, understanding how vacation enhanced family time, being together as a family the only priority. "Why did you stop going?" he asked.

"My mother shot my father and everything changed." Her voice fell flat and Alex immediately regretted asking. He quickly moved on.

"We always stayed on Okaloosa Island, just over the bridge from Destin. But we would go to Destin to have dinner at least one night." Alex felt her nostalgia and added, "We've been a few times since my dad died even though it was too painful to go without him for a long time. Then my sisters started their families and things really changed. It's just not the same. They're switching it up this year and going to Catalina Island in California instead."

"I love Catalina! I went there with friends after college. We stayed up in the hills. It reminded me of Greece. Absolutely beautiful!" her voice was animated as she talked.

"You've been to Greece?" he asked curiously.

She laughed again. "Actually no, just pictures I've seen. I've never been out of the country. How about you?"

Alex paused before answering. "I've been to Mexico, but does that really count? I've never been to Europe. Where would you like to go?" He genuinely wanted to know.

"That's easy. What girl doesn't want to go to Paris? I would do Paris and/or London, but Italy and Greece are also at the top of my wish list. How about you?"

"I guess Italy intrigues me. And Australia or New Zealand." he added, enjoying their conversation.

They walked in silence for a few moments before Chelsea stopped to take in the ocean view. Alex took the towel from around his neck and laid it on the sand. With a flourish he said, "Mademoiselle I offer you only the best seat in the house for the afternoon!"

Chelsea smiled, humoring him with a curtsey and a "thank you Monsieur!" before moving to sit down on the towel. She sipped her water, neither of them talking, just enjoying the view and the sound of the waves, their bodies close, just barely touching. It felt comfortable, Alex happy to have this time with her.

They chatted more about travel and this and that as the afternoon floated by and the sun eventually started to dip down. "We should probably get back so I can start grilling steaks."

Chelsea jumped up immediately. "Sounds like a plan to me."

They were back in no time, Chelsea setting the outdoor table and lighting candles everywhere while Alex got busy cooking dinner for the two of them. He had opened a bottle of red wine and poured a generous glass for each of them. He handed Chelsea hers as she sat in her chair taking in the sunset. It was a beautiful evening and they both appreciated it.

Dinner was relaxing and delicious as they talked about pop culture, their tastes diverse in everything but music. They both agreed old music was the best, the seventies to sing to and the eighties to dance too.

Now they sat in chairs they had carried down to the beach, a bluetooth speaker playing music between them and Chelsea wrapped in a blanket. Their wine was long gone and despite the music, she was struggling to stay awake.

"I think it's time we call it a night." Alex offered.

"I don't want to move. It's heaven right here. The music, the waves, you. It's all perfect." Chelsea said softly, her eyes closed.

For a moment Alex was tempted to stay where they were, but it was well past midnight and time to go to bed. Chelsea had let him know earlier that she had moved his suitcase to the other bedroom and he wondered now if that arrangement would stick.

"C'mon sleeping beauty. Time for bed." He pulled her reluctant body out of her chair as she groaned in protest. She leaned on him as they walked up to the house. He took her to her bed, pulling her covers back before unwrapping her from the blanket she had spent the last couple of hours in. He tucked her into bed and turned to leave when she grabbed his hand and pulled him back to her.

"Thank you Alex. I had a perfect day." she said, her eyes intent on him. "It felt good to let go of reality for the day. I needed it."

He sat down on the edge of the bed. His eyes were glowing as he gently swept her hair back from her face. "I had a perfect day with you too. We have another couple of days to enjoy. Get some sleep and I'll see you in the morning." He leaned over and kissed her gently on the cheek, her eyes already closed. "I love you Chelsea." he added softly, knowing she hadn't heard him.

He didn't even care if she did or not, it was still true. Chelsea was his one true love, but he had no idea how he was going to juggle the reality of Victoria and Chelsea. So far it had been a shit show and he wasn't sure how to make it better. In fact, he worried it would only get worse. But that was for another day. Right now he had chairs and a speaker to collect and then his own bed to crawl into. Tomorrow would be another day.

TWENTY-NINE

It had been a lovely couple of days basking in the sun and enjoying the good life. They had created a routine, both of them working on their laptops after breakfast, long walks late in the afternoon, and dinner around sunset on the large deck. With Chelsea's unspoken 'sex off the table' vibe, their relationship had a different kind of intimacy. They were getting to know each other better, talking about everything and anything under the sun during their long walks on the beach. They listened to music after dinner, late into the night over their shared bottle of wine.

Sadly it was their last day, the drive home tomorrow looming over the two of them like a wrecking ball. Chelsea's black eye had gone from bad to worse, but finally seemed to be on the mend. She would work from home the rest of the week knowing makeup would cover it nicely when she returned to the office on Monday.

Chelsea had knocked off early after Alex headed to the market for more supplies for dinner. She was enjoying his culinary skills, most impressed with the dinners he presented to her each night. She was going through her things when she came across her new two piece. She had kept Alex at arm's length the few days they had been there, but decided today was the day to break out this particular suit. It constituted very little fabric for the amount of money she had spent on it at the beginning of the summer. She checked herself in the mirror, assuming Alex would be hard pressed to resist her in this.

Alex came home to find her on her stomach, the colorful towel balanced by her white suit, the thong showcasing her back half nicely. Her face was hidden by her coverup, her smile made only to herself. She picked her head up to look at him as he pulled a chair closer to her.

"You're burning here. Do you have your sunscreen?" he asked casually enough. Surprised, she pulled it out from under her chair for him. She could feel her skin heat up as his strong hands started at her shoulders, massaging the sunscreen into her skin. He worked his way down her body, untying her top and stopping just short of coming around to her breasts. She was on fire by the time he had covered her tush and the back of her legs. Regretfully she knew her plan had backfired. She would have let him take her right then if he had just asked.

She sighed with relief as he finally finished and moved his chair back. She watched him discreetly as he unbuttoned his shirt and tossed it on the back of his chair before settling himself into it. She watched him from under her coverup as he rubbed his chest down with sunscreen. As he settled in, his eyes closed, she did her best to calm her body down, trying to ignore its need to be satisfied. She closed her eyes imagining her own happy ending, but it was hardly the same.

They sunbathed for an hour, Chelsea dozing off somewhere along the way. She woke up with a start, realizing she was alone. She sat up strategically, retying her top and shimming into her white shorts. She went inside to find Alex in the kitchen getting water bottles.

"Perfect! Time to rehydrate and go for our walk!" he announced, tossing a water bottle her way. She caught it, thankfully taking a big sip before nodding she was ready to go.

They were just about to start their walk on the beach when Alex's phone buzzed. He checked the caller id before dismissing it. When it buzzed again he apologized to Chelsea before answering it. She gathered from his side of the conversation it was Victoria with some kind of crisis that she wanted him to solve for her.

Chelsea had moved to sit back down in her chair on the deck, ready for Alex to make a mad dash back to the city and rescue Victoria. She was surprised to hear him suggest she call 911 if she were truly that concerned. It brought a smile to her lips as she could hear her losing it on the other end of the phone.

Having finished his call he turned to Chelsea expectantly, offering his arm to her with a "shall we?"

Chelsea took it, but was curious to know the back story. "Well, what traumatic event has happened in Victoria's world now?" she demanded to know.

Alex shrugged before answering nonchalantly. "Apparently she came home from her tennis lesson to discover her home had been broken into."

Chelsea stopped walking to look at him. "Are you serious? That's scary! What did they take?"

"That's just it. She can't even find anything missing. Her safe, her jewelry, her house seems untouched." Alex said, his voice annoyed.

She frowned at him. "If nothing's missing, how does she know someone broke in?"

"Exactly. I know she's dramatic and wants me to play firefighter to the fires she likes to start. That's why I suggested she call 911 if she's that concerned." He shrugged leaving it at that.

They continued down the beach, both of them lost in thought. When Chelsea released a heavy sigh, Alex gave her a look. "Let's have it. What are you thinking?"

"She wants you back Alex. Her shenanigans will continue until she gets her way and has you to herself. The fake snake on the trail, the photos, the pool. I can't compete with crazy. Which is saying something, since that used to be me. Damn you Alex, you made me soft!" She had stopped again, her tone light, but her face serious.

He took her by both arms, his face matching her seriousness. "I know she's crazy and I'm going to do my best to not enable her. She doesn't really want me back. I've told you that."

"She just doesn't want me to have you either!" Chelsea said, her voice just short of sounding bitter.

Alex turned to continue walking, his arm casually around her shoulders. "Sooner or later she's going to let it go. She's going to figure out I'm serious about you. She knows I love you and she will have to find a way to accept it. Sooner or later."

Chelsea stopped him. "But what if it's way later than anytime soon Alex? If I'm being honest, I don't know how much more I can take." She said, looking at him expectantly.

The sight of her melted him, her black eye making her seem even that much more vulnerable. He pulled her to him, holding her tight for the first time since the pool incident. "I'm in love with you Chelsea. She's my past and you're my future. There's nothing she can say or do to change that."

She broke their embrace first, nodding up at him. It felt good to hear him say it, but the truth was, she wasn't sure that was going to be enough to get them through this. She recognized a woman on a mission and at this point in the game, she would have bet on Victoria as the winner. The question was, what was she going to do about it?

THIRTY

She had showered and changed into a chartreuse slip dress, the silky fabric hugging all her curves and highlighting the tan she had deepened over the last couple of days. Alex had won the swimsuit round, but she wasn't done with him yet. She had worn the dress before and was well aware of the effect it had on him.

She accessorized her dress with a friendly smile as she joined him in the kitchen. He looked up from the boiling water long enough to glance her way. She was disappointed with his response as he turned back to the water and dropped in a couple of lobsters.

Mission accomplished, he came to stand in front of her, so close she could smell his own soapy cleanliness. She realized his hair was still wet, curling about his face in that unruly way she loved. She was surprised but stood her ground as he leaned towards her, smelling deeply into her, his breath warm on her neck.

"God you smell good. And you know what that dress does to me." he said huskily. Suddenly he pulled her close and kissed her so deep she felt it all the way down to her knees, the two of them betraying her as she had to lean into him to keep herself upright. She had missed his kisses and relished in the tingle he gave her.

Just as quickly he released her, handing her plates and silverware. "Now be a good girl and go set the table." As she turned to go he swatted her on the behind, hoping he wasn't the only one with a smile on his face.

Dinner was delicious, a plethora of fresh seafood, from the lobster to the shrimp brie toasts to the crabcakes, her absolute favorite. He had prepared her favorite summer salad, baby spinach with thinly sliced strawberries, croutons, feta, and chopped walnuts with a light vinaigrette. He had kicked it up a notch, uncorking a bottle of champagne.

When she asked him what they were celebrating he had answered simply "to us" before clicking his glass to hers. The look in his eyes had made her shiver, but she wasn't the least bit cold. They cleaned up before going to assume their usual positions in the chairs, watching the waves crash in the moonlight, the white froth the only way for them to know they were there besides the sound of them. Tonight he had pulled his chair right beside hers, taking her hand in his and holding it as they sat and talked quietly.

After three days, it appeared they had run out of things to talk about. Over the small talk, Chelsea turned on her side to face Alex, her dress revealing in this position.

"I think I'm going to turn in Alex." she said, her look direct.

"Too much champagne?" he asked, his gaze focused first on her lips before traveling down to her cleavage.

Exasperated with him she awkwardly climbed out of her chair to go and straddle him in his chair. She kissed him hard, pressing herself to him. When she released his lips she said softly, "I want you Alex. We're not leaving here without you having your way with me tonight."

She pulled herself away from him, standing expectantly in front of him. He was up in an instant, pulling her to him, his tongue moving hungrily around hers, promising of things to come. She melted into him as he picked her up and carried her inside to her bed.

Too quickly they were done, yet the night was early and laying naked together felt wonderful. Chelsea realized she had missed the cuddling as much as the sex. It was a good night and a perfect ending to their three days in The Hamptons. Tomorrow they might answer to the devil, but for tonight, it was heaven.

THIRTY-ONE

They were back on the Long Island Expressway, the city sure to be upon them soon. After a long night of making love, Chelsea had dozed off for a quick nap. She felt relaxed and happy, but wondered how long it could last once they were back within Victoria's treacherous reach. She had given a lot of thought to how she was going to handle the situation and make it work for her and Alex. No matter how she spun it, it seemed she would need to talk to Victoria. She had a proposal to make and assumed Victoria would accept it.

Realizing she was finally awake, Alex put his hand on her leg and asked, "What world problem are you solving over there?"

She laughed and queried back, "What makes you think I'm solving world problems?"

He glanced her way, "Now I know you are because you're stalling. Care to share?"

Chelsea stared out the window, answering briefly, "No thank you."

"Fine. What do you plan to do first when I drop you at home?" he asked, knowing it would be useless to push her.

"That's easy. I'm going to go for a long run and work off all your delicious dinners I enjoyed this week." she smiled as she said it. "How about you?"

Technically it was still a work day and she had a pretty good idea of what Alex would say. "I'll stop by the office and see what fires can't wait until tomorrow." He glanced her way before asking. "Are you running through the park?"

"Of course!" she added not thinking it through.

She saw his look go grim. "Please promise me you'll be careful."

Chelsea swallowed hard, reminded that she had never confessed how she had come to be mugged. She focused her gaze out the window feeling like she should come clean with Alex. She sighed as she opened the can of worms, their first reality check as they moved closer to the city skyline.

"I know I never told you this, but I was mugged in the subway thingy. I wasn't in the park."

Seeing his look of confusion, she pressed on. "I was finishing my run at the park when I noticed a woman who reminded me of Victoria. For just a moment I thought it was her. Anyway I was curious about the woman and followed her down into the subway. When everyone got on the train, I was alone and that's when the guy popped up out of nowhere."

He kept his eyes on the road as Chelsea waited for him to say something, but all he said was "I see." A few minutes passed before he added, "Tell me about your plan to handle Victoria." He glanced her way before adding, "And don't bother to deny you have one, because I know you do."

Chelsea took a deep breath before answering. "I'm curious who Victoria's mother is. And now I want to know if she has a sister. Maybe embracing her new family would take some of her time and attention off of us."

"And how do you plan to go about finding out something that is really none of your business?" His voice was controlled, but she could still feel his annoyance with her.

"When someone is trying to ruin your life, it becomes my business and they should know you're going to fight back. I hired a private investigator. I hope to know something by the end of the week."

"What else?" he asked, this time letting his gaze meet hers, daring her to deny there was more.

"I plan to recruit one of the junior editors to take over Victoria's book. She will reoffer what I've already presented to her and hopefully she will accept it and we can all move forward with getting this thing in print."

Alex looked doubtful. "She's going to know you're the one behind the work, the said editor will be just a mouthpiece."

Chelsea looked at him exasperated. "What do you want me to do Alex? Do you want to handle all the details? All the fine print? Does she want *Deathbed* published or not?!"

He relented then. "I know, you're right. We do need a plan. It's all very personal, but to be clear it's also about business. For over a decade I've busted my ass to make Hudson & Butler a force to be reckoned with in publishing. I won't jeopardize losing it!"

Chelsea stared at him, for the first time feeling his frustration with the situation at hand. She hadn't thought about it from that angle, seeing it only as a personal attack on her and the relationship they shared.

"I get it Alex. I'll do whatever you want me to do. I don't want to make anything worse. I'm just trying to find a way to help us all move forward and come out in one piece."

He took her hand laying on the console and raised it to his lips. "I know. Just tread lightly. I want to know what you're up to, what you find out, I want to be kept in the loop. Understand?"

She nodded, looking him in the face before turning her focus back to the window, watching the buildings of Manhattan float by her. "Alex, why don't you ask her which junior editor she's comfortable with and then I'll catch them up to speed. I promise to be discreet."

He nodded before pulling up in front of her building. He jumped out of the car to retrieve her bag. She looked at him with a smile. "Thank you for a great week. It was just what I needed."

He sat her bag down and pulled her to him, kissing her deeply. "You're welcome. I'll be back later." I hope so, Chelsea thought to herself, I hope so.

THIRTY-TWO

She smiled at the housekeeper as she opened the door, announcing she was there to see Victoria. Assuming she was not welcome in her home, Chelsea raised her hand to silence her knock adding she wanted to surprise her. The girl gave a nod and left her to it.

Chelsea knocked respectfully not wanting to startle Victoria. As she had crisply demanded, she went into the room, ready to be admonished.

Seeing her frown, Chelsea spoke first. "Hello Victoria. I thought we should talk. Do you have a minute?"

"How did you get in my house?" she demanded.

"I talked your housekeeper into letting me in unannounced but that's only because I thought you wouldn't let me in and I really need to talk to you." Chelsea said.

"And of course whatever you want, you just expect to get. I don't know how many times I can say I never want to see you again!" She stood at her desk, her body bristling with outrage.

Chelsea dismissed her with a wave adding, "You'll want to hear this believe me. It can solve a lot of our problems. Chelsea went to lay a couple of files on her desk before retreating to a chair across from it.

Ignoring Victoria's refusal to pick up the files, Chelsea launched into explaining them to her anyway. "This is the work I've given the junior editor to make sure your book is the best it can be before it goes to print."

Victoria sat down with a thud. "I don't know how many times I can say this. I want *Alex* to handle my book. It's the least he can do after all I've done for him!"

Chelsea frowned. "You've done for him? Oh you mean writing a check to start a business that has earned you ten times that amount of money for little to no work on your part? Editing isn't what Alex does at Hudson & Butler and you know it!" In her head she could hear Alex warning her to tread lightly.

She relented, taking a nicer approach. "Of course Alex wants your book to be everything you want it to be. He supports you in that one hundred percent, but he is not an editor or the one to manage the net-working for your book. I know you know that Victoria, why else would you have let him grow the multi-million dollar business that he has. You know where his strengths lie."

Her tone was icy as Victoria said, "What else?"

Chelsea crossed her legs, plunging into the contents of the second folder. "I think you should find out who your real mother is. Victoria, you need someone else in your life. I don't know what it's like, but I can imagine how much you must miss your mother. All the pranks, the accusations, I get it. You're bored, you're lonely, you hate me, but we all know you don't *really* want Alex back."

She paused, watching Victoria search for the words that were sure to come. "And what is your excuse for the obnoxious pranks you've pulled Chelsea? The rubber snake to startle my horse during my ride? The photos of you and Alex to rub your relationship in my face?"

Chelsea's eyes narrowed. "That's just it. I didn't plant the snake or the photos and you know it!"

"Then who did? Who else would have a reason to go to such vin-dictive moves?' Who? I want to know!" She all but screamed.

Chelsea remained calm despite bristling over her accusations.

"Think about it Victoria. What do I stand to gain from pulling shit like that? But if it wasn't either one of us, then I think I might know who."

Seeing Victoria's doubtful look, she went to the desk and pulled out a picture of a woman. She handed the picture to her, curious to what her reaction would be. She didn't have to wait long.

Victoria took in a sharp breath before demanding, "Where did you get this? And why do you have it? Is this another sick prank of yours?" Her shock at seeing the picture was undeniable.

"Do you recognize her? I saw her at the park and took her picture?" Chelsea said.

"But why would you take her picture? Why would you bring me a picture of her? Do *you* know her?" her questions came quickly.

"How would I know her? But isn't it obvious why I took it?" Chelsea demanded back. As a sudden afterthought, she said, "Do *you* know her?"

Victoria studied the picture for a minute, before answering. "I do." Seeing Chelsea's surprised look she added. "I would swear this is our old housekeeper's daughter, Rory. We were best friends when we were little. For awhile there we were almost like sisters"

Chelsea was floored. "Were best friends?" she asked softly.

She shrugged before answering. "We got older and of course went to different schools. You know how it is. I was busy hanging out with my school friends."

They both jumped at the shrill sound of the telephone on Victoria's desk. She glanced at Chelsea briefly before picking it up with an abrupt "Yes?"

Chelsea watched her face, realizing it was not good news. She waited patiently for the conversation to end.

As she hung up the phone, her voice was quiet as she announced, "My father was hit by a car and he's in a coma." She stood suddenly. "I need to get to the hospital. Now!"

Chelsea stood up too, "My driver is waiting right outside. We can take you. You shouldn't be driving."

Victoria nodded numbly, following Chelsea to the door. In no time they were in the car headed to the hospital. Chelsea had offered to call Alex and he was quick to agree he would meet them there.

They both stared out their respective windows, lost in their own thoughts, the city crawling by as traffic demanded.

"It's hard to know how to feel, isn't it?" Chelsea asked suddenly.

"What?" Victoria asked her blankly.

"It's hard to know how to feel." she repeated. "It's your father after all, but he's someone you usually hate. But now that his life is in danger, it's your *father* and it's hard to dismiss that.

Victoria looked annoyed. "Don't try to be my friend now. Like you could possibly know how I feel."

"When my mother shot my father, there was a part of me that wished he would die. It was a horrible thought, but he was so hateful to us both. But the other part of me was desperate for him to be okay. For all of us to be okay." Chelsea cut to the chase, not mincing her words. "But I was eleven and you're a grown woman so maybe you're right, how would I know how you're feeling? And maybe your father was an amazing father."

Victoria snorted before answering her. "Yeah right! My mother and I always knew work was his first love, his first priority, even though he would tell us he did it all for us. Bullshit! I guess you're right. It is hard to know how to feel. Was your father okay?"

Chelsea shrugged. "He was, but he sent my mother away to rehab for a good six months. The longest six months of my life. If it hadn't been for our housekeeper, I would have shriveled up and blown away. She and another friend got me through it."

Victoria nodded. "My mom struggled with her mental health for as long as I can remember. Our housekeeper was like a second mother to me. She more than took care of me. I knew she loved me too."

Chelsea was startled to hear her words. She thought back to their conversation, right before the phone rang. How ironic she knew the woman in the photo as her "old housekeeper's daughter."

Chelsea looked at her curiously. "Did you stay in touch with her? Do you know where she is now?"

Victoria shook her head. "The last time I saw her was over a year ago at my mother's funeral. But I hadn't seen her in years before that. Why do you ask?"

Chelsea went back to the safety of her window. "No reason, just making conversation." This wasn't the time for it, but definitely it would be in the near future. But first, to the hospital to find out more about what had happened to Victoria's father. And would he live? All she could think about was it really was hard to know how to feel.

THIRTY-THREE

It had been twenty-four hours since Victoria got the call about her father and all hell broke loose. Her father was on life support and highly unlikely to survive once Victoria signed the form to authorize pulling the plug. Despite her professed hatred of the man, she had yet to agree to sign anything. Chelsea understood the pressure to stand alone as an only child, her mother already gone, and having to make such a hard decision.

The other nugget had been that witnesses of her father getting hit by the car had revealed some devastating news. After talking with several witnesses, everyone seemed to think he had been targeted. The big news had been that the car's description matched the description of the car that Victoria owned. Only one witness had taken the first three digits of the plates which had matched Victoria's plates. It seemed she was a suspect until the police had gone to her home to collect the car and discovered it was already gone. Despite her protests that it had been stolen without her realizing it, she appeared to be the number one suspect in her own father's hit and run.

Chelsea watched from afar as Victoria dealt with it all, Alex right by her side. She knew he was struggling, checking in with her often while staying by Victoria's side. Now it had been decided that Victoria should stay with Alex in his guest room, his apartment much closer to the hospital than her drive to a huge empty house all the way to Brooklyn. Needless to say, Chelsea had mixed feelings about this.

Chelsea tossed and turned all night, searching for what to do before coming to a painful realization. Coming fully awake she could hear the shower running and impulsively got out of bed and went to join Alex, hopeful he wasn't in a big hurry.

He looked surprised when she opened the door, but quickly recovered and greeted her with a "Morning beautiful."

She couldn't help but smile, appreciating his lie, knowing her bed hair alone would be the first piece of evidence to prove him wrong. She went to join him in the shower, answering him back with a 'morning handsome" before putting her arms around his neck and kissing him long and hard.

They were both quickly lathered up, enjoying the intimacy of massaging soap into each other's naked bodies before moving on to the more serious business of satisfying each other. Chelsea was the first to pull their towels from the towel warmer, handing Alex his before wrapping her own around herself. She gave him one last kiss before moving on to getting dressed and facing the rest of their day.

They rode the elevator up to Hudson & Butler holding hands, Alex raising her hand to his lips as the elevator doors opened. Chelsea smiled and mouthed 'love you' before they each headed to their own offices. Chelsea knew she had chickened out of telling Alex she would be staying at her own apartment for a while, giving him the space he needed to help Victoria through letting her father go. She had no doubt it would be a long road ahead, sadly for all of them.

She glanced around at the plethora of manuscripts sprawled across her bed, sighing loudly. Dreading the weekend that stretched out before her, she had selected four to five manuscripts to bring home with her. She was willing to spend her weekend reading, searching for the perfect manuscript to begin the publishing process with. While she knew Hudson & Butler had a large staff more than competent to carry out their assigned tasks they were hired for, she struggled to delegate any of the publishing tasks to others.

From the beginning, she had made it clear she wanted to be the one to move the author's manuscript from beginning to end. She had been with the company just long enough that people were starting to give her the creative license she demanded, but also the respect for how she gave each book she handled a life of its own.

As of last month, she was responsible for getting four books on The New York Time's Best Seller List in the last nine months. She was working her ass off to launch her new authors into the limelight, while also getting her own name out there. Occasionally a wannabe author would personally request her to read their manuscript, hoping she would work her magic for them as well.

She lay back into her pillows, unable to make a selection. She let herself be distracted, checking her phone for activity. It was hard for her to believe her life had been near perfection just mere months ago. She and Alex had been so happy, so in love, living the dream both professionally and personally.

Somehow they had taken a sharp detour when Alex's ex had brought them her manuscript for publication. As someone who had perfected manipulating all sorts of people, Chelsea had known she was in for a challenge when she first said hello to Victoria. She had immediately recognized her look of desperate woman on a mission, and understood how it had become directed at her.

Chelsea checked the weather and then the time, disappointed to find nothing of interest on her phone. She marveled at how social media could connect people in their daily lives and yet, the lonely remained behind the scenes, feeling more isolated than ever. She hated that feeling of knowing her agenda was wide open for the weekend yet again.

She reopened her latest text from Kat, thankful and relieved she would fly in for a quick visit next week. She had baited her with the need to review her numbers and start planning the launch for her newest book. Towards the end of their conversation, she had casually mentioned to Kat that they should go out. When Kat had asked her "go out where?" Chelsea told her to bring her dancing shoes, it was time for them to hit a club. There was no clubbing like clubbing in New York City. If she played her cards right, she would have enough fun Friday night to get her through some lonely weekends ahead.

THIRTY-FOUR

Chelsea squeezed Kat's hand in excited anticipation as the car service moved them slowly through downtown traffic, the two of them headed to the Hotel 50 Bowery, a boutique hotel in the heart of lower Manhattan. The plan was to have some drinks at The Crown, the Bowery's rooftop bar, before heading down to Daphne in the basement for some dancing. Both women were dressed to the nines, but Chelsea liked to think her sparkle was just a little brighter and more polished than Kat's.

They were soon seated at the bar, Chelsea ordering the house specialty drink for both of them. The Light My Fire cocktail was made with Casamigos tequila, honey, ginger and fresh lime. The bartender had offered to add flamed rosemary to their drink if they were feeling feisty. Both women passed, Chelsea realizing she was feeling feisty enough without it. They sipped their cocktails, admiring their view of the Manhattan skyline, the sunset making it appear almost magical. Chelsea gave a big smile to their bartender as he sat down a plate of pan fried chicken dumplings between the two of them. She never drank on an empty stomach and happily woofed down her fair share.

The bar was fairly full and Chelsea surveyed the selection of men rather passively. She wasn't looking to hook up, but rather to just have some fun and let loose on a Friday night. She was sure dancing was just what she needed both mentally and physically. Meanwhile Kat worked to make small talk with Chelsea, catching her up on her and Thomas's personal life. It never occurred to her that Kat was struggling to find common ground between the two of them, their conversation avoiding the elephant in the room. Eventually Kat could avoid it no longer.

"So, what's up with you and Alex? What happened between the two of you anyway?" Kat asked bravely.

It was not lost on Kat that Chelsea struggled to compose herself before answering the question.

She went with a flip answer first. "Alex who? Just kidding. It turns out Alex is still more attached to his ex-wife than he had imagined. She's going through a tough time and I stepped out of the picture to make it easier for both of them. I'm a saint now or haven't you already heard?" She ended with a bitter laugh, her sarcasm not lost on Kat.

Kat wasn't sure how to answer. "No way. I've seen you two together. You were meant for each other. Did you give Alex a choice or did you just walk away?"

Chelsea shrugged. "I made the choice for both of us. Hard as hell for me, but easier for him!" She sighed heavily before sipping her drink. "Don't worry about me though, I'll be fine. Eventually." Chelsea added the last part, her voice breaking ever so slightly, showing her true emotions.

Chelsea could not handle the sympathy in Kat's eyes. Impulsively she jumped up, grabbing Ka't hand. "Time to go dance my friend! The night is young!" A little apprehensive, Kat followed her, headed to the basement better known as Daphne.

THIRTY-FIVE

The girls had been on the dance floor multiple times, Chelsea loving the shimmer of the disco balls. Kat had to admit it was fun to dance to classics from the seventies, while still enjoying the DJ's bump and grind. She could feel herself getting a little tipsy, but realizing Chelsea was well lit, had slowed her roll. She noticed they, or rather Chelsea, had attracted the attention of a couple of men, and she blanched when magically shots of vodka showed up at their table.

Chelsea eagerly picked up first one and then the other, raising her vodka in a toast to the men before slamming both shots down. It wasn't long before the two men approached the girls, asking them to dance. Chelsea grabbed Kat's arm as she headed to the dance floor, the men following behind them.

An hour passed by painfully for Kat, the shots flowing and Chelsea's dance moves getting sloppier with every song. Kat started to wonder how the night was going to end, her concern for Chelsea growing as one of the men became increasingly more possessive with her. Not knowing what else to do, she made a quick phone call, hoping he would pick up, despite the lateness of the hour.

Suddenly Chelsea was at her elbow, her words slurred as she announced they were invited to a party at the penthouse suite of the hotel. Kat knew she was going to have to stand her ground and stall as Chelsea linked her arm in hers, trying to drag her off her barstool.

Kat turned to face both Chelsea and the two men head on. "Chelsea, you know it's getting late and we have a very early call in the morning. Sorry, but we're going to have to pass on that, but thank you!" Kat said, trying to sound firm with her polite decline on behalf of both of them.

Chelsea put her arm around Kat's neck and pulled her close enough to talk in her ear. "I'm trying to ditch them, but they're not getting the hint. Follow my lead."

"C'mon Kat, just one drink upstairs and we'll call it a night!" As Chelsea moved away, dragging Kat with her, she suddenly paused dramatically, bending over, her hand to her head.

"Kat, I don't feel so good! I think I'm gonna be sick! I need a bathroom!" Chelsea suddenly gave a little shriek as her dance partner grabbed her up under the arm, heading her toward the elevators.

"I have just what you need to take care of that." he said with a leer, giving a nod to the other one to grab Kat.

Kat frantically looked to the bartender for help, noticing he had suddenly busied himself at the far end of the bar. She turned to Chelsea just as she threw up all over one of the men's high dollar wingtips. Kat moved to stand by her as he started to yell obscenities at her.

"You bitch! You did that on purpose!" His hand gripped her arm tighter. "You're going to pay for that!"

As the men wrestled the girls towards the elevator, they came up short as another angry man got off yelling. "What the hell are you doing down here?" It was Alex, his demeanor hostile towards Chelsea. "I apologize if my wife is causing you gentlemen any trouble." he added, turning towards the man holding onto her.

"Your wife? Your wife?" He paused, assessing which way he wanted to play the situation at hand. Kat held her breath anxiously, waiting to see.

"You can have your wife! She's a bore of a bitch anyway, but she owes me. She just ruined my very expensive shoes!" The man held onto Chelsea, clearly not backing down.

Kat noticed Chelsea really wasn't looking well and then turned in shock as Alex handed the man a wad of hundred dollar bills.

"That should take care of your shoes. Now hand my drunk of a wife over so we can get the hell out of here!" Alex went to take Chelsea's arm as the man took Alex's money, Kat quickly moving to her other arm. She didn't need any urging to hit the elevator button, feeling most thankful when it magically slid open immediately, closing just as the men turned to follow them.

Kat was thankful to sink into the leather seat of Alex's car service, wanting to be as far away as possible from their current situation. Chelsea had passed out in no time, her head resting on Alex's shoulder.

Alex sat fuming for a good couple of blocks before he finally turned to Kat and demanded, "What the hell happened tonight Kat?"

"She wanted to go dancing. She needed to have some fun." Kat said defensively.

"I've never seen her drunk. It's almost like she's drugged!" Kat watched Alex try to wake Chelsea up, a realization hitting her hard.

"Oh my god! Do you think one of them roofied her drink?" Kat asked horrified.

"You tell me Kat! Or was she really drinking a lot?" he asked, his tone flat.

Kat nodded her answer to Alex, not able to look him in the eyes. "I've never seen her drink like that, but she went hard tonight. Too many vodka shots to count. I'm sorry Alex."

Alex answered her a little more kindly. "Why are you sorry? Chelsea is a grown woman. I'm glad you called me though. You're both lucky to be out of there in one piece."

Alex turned to Chelsea, checking her pulse worriedly. "I've never seen her drink more than two drinks ever. She's the queen of nursing a cocktail."

Kat rubbed her head as it started to throb, her own shots starting to catch up to her. "You can say a lot of things about Chelsea, but she's definitely not a lush. I guess that's what happens when your mother is an alcoholic."

Months ago the girls had bonded over growing up with an alcoholic in the house. In Kat's house it had been her dad, a gentle drunk, but still unable to hold a job or be depended on most of the time. For Chelsea it had been her mother.

Kat suddenly realized Alex had turned his attention to her and was staring at her. "You know her mother was an alcoholic?"

Kat nodded cautiously.

Reflectively Alex took Chelsea's hand, his thumb rubbing the top of it. "So why all the shots tonight? Why was she being so reckless?"

Kat looked at him incredulously. "You tell me Alex? Why do you think?" she said, trying to keep the frustration out of her voice.

She watched as his face went from confusion to the realization of just how much Chelsea was hurting. "She made the choice for both of us. I would have played it a different way, but she didn't bother to ask me." he said gruffly.

He turned to Kat. "I'm glad she has a friend like you. Thank god you were there for her tonight. Thank you."

Kat couldn't hide her surprise before answering him back. "Whoa! I'm glad I could be there for her too, but we aren't friends. That would be a stretch!"

Alex looked at Kat intently. "Really? I didn't realize you're at capacity in the friends department. You're watching out for her, defending her, seem to know her secrets, what would you call that?"

Kat looked away, unable to handle his challenging gaze. "Fine, I guess we are friends. You're right, but damn it's a big job!"

Alex laughed softly. "You should try being her lover." He quickly added, "Thank you Kat, clearly she needs a friend, someone she can trust. I'm glad she has you. And just so you know, I love her. I will always need her in my life."

As they reached Kat's hotel and she went to climb out of the car, she turned back to look at him. "Then why does she seem to think she's second fiddle Alex? And I'm not the one you need to tell. Make sure she knows you love her and she's your first priority. Take care of her Alex."

He gave Kat a nod, before turning back to Chelsea's limp body. He leaned his head back on the head rest and stared out the window as the car pulled away. Loving Chelsea was harder some days than others, but he realized he wasn't willing to let her go. He knew now he shouldn't have let her walk away so easily and fought harder for them. He and Chelsea both knew he had his hands full with Victoria. He could only hope it wasn't too late to get Chelsea back. Carrying her upstairs to his penthouse, he knew it was nothing that would be solved tonight.

THIRTY-SIX

Alex stood in the doorway sipping his second cup of coffee, watching Chelsea sleep. He regretted the hell she was going to feel when she finally came too. Despite last night's makeup and his oversized t-shirt she slept in, she looked beautiful to him, even if it was in a fragile kind of way at the moment. He came out of his reverie as she stirred, her hand quickly moving to her head.

"Oh my god, why is someone pounding on my head? Please for the love of god make it stop!" Chelsea moaned.

Alex walked to her, sitting gingerly on the side of the bed. "Afternoon sunshine. It's nice of you to join us." he said softly.

Chelsea turned her gaze on him, surprised to see him, let alone be sleeping in his bed.

"Alex. What am I doing here? What happened last night?" Chelsea asked, struggling to function.

"You somehow let vodka get the best of you and then I had to rescue you and Kat from some very serious predators. I was concerned about your level of intoxication, so I brought you here so I could take care of you."

"You rescued us? Is Kat okay?" Chelsea's voice trembled with emotion.

"She is. Thankfully she recognized that you two were in way over your heads and decided to call me. If I hadn't arrived when I did, you both might have got something much worse than a dance party last night." His voice was gentle, but he needed Chelsea to know how reckless she had been.

He watched as the night's events started to come back to her. "The Russians! I threw up on some very expensive Prada shoes. I was trying to distract him." She finished weakly.

"He wasn't having it until I shoved a wad of cash in his hand. We were lucky the elevator doors opened when they did. Chelsea, what were you thinking?"

Chelsea closed her eyes, unable to look at Alex. "I was thinking I needed to have some fun and forget for a little while how much I miss you." she whispered.

Gently Alex brought Chelsea up to him, holding her to him tightly. "When Kat called, practically hysterical, I was scared for you both!"

She was quiet as he laid her back into her pillows. "Are you ready for something to eat? Some coffee? Advil? An ice pack?" It felt good to see how much he wanted to take care of her.

"Food no, coffee yes please. And maybe some advil." Chelsea closed her eyes again, fighting the wave of nausea at the thought of food.

She was thankful when Alex quickly returned with her coffee, noting that he had made it just the way she liked it, strong and black with just a shot of creamer. She let him fuss over her, his warm hands on her giving her a different set of problems. She watched him as she sipped her coffee, wondering to herself if Victoria were in the apartment and if she knew Chelsea was there.

She had mixed feelings about being there, knowing this was a temporary reprieve. Taking a deep breath, she finally asked about Victoria, not wanting to accidentally run into her once she left the safety of Alex's bedroom. It surprised her to learn Victoria was already back in Brooklyn, having only stayed for a week or so. She wasn't going to get her hopes up though. She knew Victoria would always need Alex and Chelsea had never been good at sharing. For now, she was going to work to survive her hangover and worry about the logistics of their relationship tomorrow.

It was getting late in the day and she was starting to feel human again, mortified that a day of her life had passed her by. She had never been able to understand how her mother could drink so much, just to feel like shit physically and emotionally afterwards.

They sat on Alex's couch having just finished P.J.'s burgers and fries, apparently a classic cure for any hangover. Chelsea had been guzzling water all afternoon like it was going out of style. They were pretending to watch a movie, but she knew a hard conversation was brewing. She waited for Alex to begin. She could feel his gaze on her, his look intense.

"Now that we know you've survived your battle with Vodka, I have some questions." She turned her gaze to him, but said nothing. "Why did you move your things out Chelsea? I wasn't trading you for Victoria." He waited for her answer.

"What did you think was going to happen when she moved in?" Her voice was quiet as she asked him, curious to know.

"I *thought* we were in a relationship. A relationship strong enough to survive me helping a friend." his voice was hard and Chelsea realized she had hurt him.

"I didn't mean to hurt you Alex. I was trying to make it easy for you. And Victoria is not just a friend. She's your ex-wife who is going through a lot right now and she needs you. All of you."

"Should I have asked for your permission first before asking her to stay here?" His voice was a little bitter, showing his frustration with the situation at hand.

Chelsea stood up and started to pace in front of the couch. "Of course not! Don't you get it? I love you and I'm trying to help make this horrible situation easier for you. You and Victoria have a history and let's face it, she's always going to need you! You're always going to care about her and feel like you're responsible for her. I can't compete with that!" She was distraught, trying to make him see the logic behind her move.

He stood up and came to her, pulling her to him and holding her tightly. He knew she was right. They were stuck in an impossible situation, this emotional three way circus a situation neither of them knew how to handle. He led her back to the couch, pulling the two of them down to sit together.

"Please don't be mad at me Alex." she mumbled, her head on his shoulder. They sat together for a moment or two, each of them lost in their own thoughts. If ever there was a time to share her plan with Alex, she knew now was the perfect opportunity.

She pulled away to look at him. "Tell me what's happening with her case? Has it been dismissed yet? Do they have any other leads?" She knew Victoria had pulled the plug and her father was gone. She knew the funeral was scheduled for the end of next week. She could imagine how difficult it all must be, but she could not imagine wondering who would deliberately run her father down. Chelsea had a few thoughts about it.

Alex shook his head before answering her. "For now there seem to be no answers. She still seems to be the number one suspect. Her arraignment is in a couple of weeks. Her lawyer doesn't seem too concerned, but if there are no other suspects I can't imagine they would just let it go."

Chelsea watched Alex, his expression serious. "Are they even searching for another suspect?" she asked.

"They're saying her inheritance is grounds for motive, but her father would have given her anything she asked for."

"I think I know someone else who might have had a motive." She stood up as he could only stare at her stunned. "But I need you to take me to my apartment. Then I can explain." Just like that they were headed out the door.

THIRTY-SEVEN

She had her key in the door, when they heard a small crash within the apartment. Immediately Alex stepped in front of her, putting his finger to his lips, signaling for her to be quiet. She nodded, happy to let him take the lead. The lights were off except for sporadic flashes of light coming from Chelsea's spare bedroom she had set up like an office. The door was ajar and they tiptoed to it. As Alex swung the door open, they were both shocked to see who the intruder was.

Chelsea flipped on the light while at the same time demanding, "Victoria what the hell do you think you're doing?!"

She whirled around from the desk drawer she was rifling through, just as shocked to see them. They all stood frozen for a moment, none of them sure what to do next. As Chelsea went to move forward, the intruder grabbed the large exercise ball near the desk and threw it at the two of them. She ran from the room as they dodged the ball, hurdling herself down the hallway.

Alex was the first to go after her, Chelsea not far behind. They were astounded to make it back to the hallway only to discover she had magically disappeared. Alex looked at Chelsea, his hands on his hips, his face thunderous. "What the hell just happened here?"

He followed Chelsea back into the apartment. "Why do you not seem as shocked as I am to see her? And why did that woman look like Victoria, but could not possibly have been her?"

Chelsea motioned to Alex to stay where he was while announcing at the same time, "I know what she was after!"

She came back into the room in no time, her expression triumphant, holding a manilla envelope. "This is what she was looking for. She started in my office, but we both know I do my best work in bed!"

Alex looked puzzled. "I don't get it. What's in your envelope?"

"Have you ever seen Victoria dressed like a cat burglar? That woman didn't come in the front door of the building either. But look for yourself!" She said, handing him the envelope.

He took the envelope to her coffee table and dumped the contents after plopping down on the couch. He flipped through them rapidly as Chelsea continued to explain.

"Remember when I got mugged because I followed that woman that looked like Victoria into the subway? I wanted to know more about her and hired a private investigator." Seeing him look up at her sharply, she hastily added, "I told you I would! Remember?"

He dropped the photos and leaned back on the couch. "I remember asking why you would pursue something like that when it has nothing to do with you."

Chelsea nodded, quick to reply. "And I said Victoria made it my business when she started making bullshit accusations."

"Go on." Alex said brusquely.

"He had to do some digging, but he found out who the woman is. He actually found out more than I could imagine. It cost me a small fortune, but I needed to know. Actually we ALL need to know." she added the end dramatically.

Alex rolled his eyes, his patience wearing thin. "Get to the point Chelsea. Who is she? And what do we all need to know?"

Chelsea bent down to pick up one of the photos that had haunted her the most. The woman was sitting in the window of a well known lunch spot in Brooklyn, dressed to the nines. When she was dressed like this, there was no denying her relationship to Victoria. She took a deep breath before announcing,

"The woman is Victoria's sister Rory. Her twin to be exact!" She held the photo up for Alex to see for himself.

He took it from her, taking a closer look. He glanced up at Chelsea before tossing it back on the coffee table. He stood up, running his hand through his hair, a sure sign he was distressed.

Finally Chelsea could stand it no longer. "Well? Do you not believe me?" she asked flatly.

He came to stand in front of her, his face serious. "I believe you, but will Victoria believe it? And will this news make her or break her? And when I say her, you know who I mean."

Chelsea nodded, her expression now worried. "You mean us!"

"There's more, isn't there?" he asked.

She nodded. "I went to see Victoria the day her father got hit by a car. I had a picture of the woman from my phone and I showed it to her. She wanted to know why I would take it, not even realizing the resemblance to herself. She asked me if I knew the woman and something in her expression made me ask her if she knew the woman. She said she reminded her of her housekeeper's daughter whom she grew up playing with. Said they were like sisters until they both started school. They went to different schools and well, you know the rest."

Alex looked incredulous, his voice somber. "So you're telling me that if that woman is Victoria's twin, then the housekeeper she grew up with, the woman who took care of her as much if not more than her own mother, is actually her biological mother?"

When Chelsea nodded yes, he could only say, "Damn!"

His hands were running through his hair again as he went back to sit down on her couch. Chelsea watched his face as a range of emotions flitted across it. Finally he looked up at Chelsea to ask, "How are we going to tell her this? And when? Before or after she buries her father? Before or after her arraignment?"

Listening to Alex ask the hard questions, she realized that Victoria would need Alex now more than ever to be there for her. But she also had an epiphany that Alex was going to need to lean on Chelsea to get Victoria through it all. She went to sit on the couch beside Alex and took his hand, squeezing it hard.

"It's going to be rough, but you'll be there for Victoria and I'll be here for you." she said softly.

Alex studied her, his gaze intense. "Are you sure about that? No trips off to greener pastures?"

Chelsea frowned. "What do you mean by that?" she asked cautiously.

He stood up abruptly before turning back to her. "I know about your Paris trip. Victoria loved breaking the news to me, a bright spot in her otherwise shitty world." His voice was harsh, making Chelsea cringe inwardly.

Damn that bitch! She stood up too, going to stand in front of him. "I asked her to let me be the one to tell you once I knew she would sign off her approval for my plan."

"What the hell Chelsea! I laughed in her face and didn't believe her when she told me. I thought it was another attempt to make you look bad, but oh no, she was more than happy to pull up your email. Why didn't you come to me with the plan?"

Chelsea stood her ground, facing his wrath head on. "I didn't come to you because I was afraid you would try to talk me out of it! I was afraid you would flat out say no! But I'm not going anytime soon. And it's only for seven weeks which will fly by!" Chelsea realized she was crumbling under his look of disbelief. "I'm going to be here for you Alex. I promise I won't go until you're ready."

Alex picked up one of the photos still laying on her coffee table and tucked it inside his jacket. His voice was flat as he turned to her one more time. "I think Victoria is more likely to believe me if I tell her alone. I don't know what her new found sister is up to, but it's going to be a lot for her to learn she has a twin sister and has known her mother all along after all. Thanks for your help. I'll take it from here."

With that he turned on his heel and was out her door. Chelsea followed him to the door, wanting to say something that would make it better for both of them. She leaned against the slammed door, sliding to the bottom of it knowing there was nothing she could say. But one thing she did know was. Like hell he would get to handle it from here without her.

THIRTY-EIGHT

She sat in the middle of the bed, photos and papers spread out everywhere. She had been so focused on her Paris project that she had really never gone through the full contents of the envelope. At some point, she had glanced through all the photos, but neglected to take a close look. It was still early evening, but she had showered and was dressed in her favorite navy velour tracksuit, ready to focus all of her attention on the task at hand.

She ordered the photos by their dates first, hoping it would tell a story of Victoria's new found sister. The woman was dressed down in many of the photos, usually wearing black jeans and black hoodies. She picked up the one that had haunted her the most, the one of her dressed to the nines, sitting at a window table at a very popular lunch spot in DUMBO. As she stared at the photo, Chelsea suddenly realized why this photo had grabbed her attention. Looking closer at the photo, she realized that she had seen Victoria in the very same dress for one of their meetings. It was the red sheath dress and would be memorable on most anyone.

She glanced out the window as a large crack of thunder made her jump. She was deep in thought, remembering Victoria's phone call to Alex that her house had been broken into. Had it actually been her sister taking no more than clothes from her closet? She stared at the photo in disbelief. It was then that something else caught her eye. The woman was holding a coffee cup, but it was the way she held the mug that caught Chelsea's attention.

Shaking her head, she exclaimed, "No way!" She got her phone to take another photo so she could zoom in to take a closer look.

"What the hell?" she asked herself, her voice alarmed. Frantically she searched through other photos, hoping it was a fluke. To her dismay she found two other photos with the same situation. She shook her head in disbelief, but could not deny the woman was flipping off the photographer, her hired PI. It was discreet, but her message was clear. I see you and don't give two shits.

Chelsea leaned back into her bed pillows stunned. Somehow Victoria's sister had made out her private investigator and was letting them know she knew he was there. No wonder she had broken into her apartment looking for the photos. Thankfully she had not found them. She pulled out the paperwork, knowing she should have taken a look a week ago when the PI had first handed it to her.

She carefully perused the ten page report, full of disheartening details. Victoria's sister had experienced a troubled youth, acquiring a short rap sheet before she had even graduated from a high school on Staten Island. After graduation she enlisted in the army. Chelsea wasn't surprised she had made the most common military choice for high school graduates, but was still impressed she had survived the physical and mental demands of basic training. She had climbed the ranks quickly and served for a number of years in Iraq. Reading on, Chelsea was dismayed to learn that at some point she had been served a dishonorable discharge from the army. Chelsea wondered what had happened to send her home.

As she kept reading, the real kicker came when she found a document labeled "confidential" at the bottom of the report. Chelsea was alarmed to find a variety of mental diagnosis from ADHD to bipolar disorder. The document revealed her mood swings, apparently leading to occasional violent outbursts, most likely leading to her discharge.

It suddenly made sense to Chelsea the unexplained shenanigans that had contributed to the hostile relationship between herself and Victoria. She had to wonder what was her motivation to go to the trouble to wreak such havoc. More importantly she wondered at what point she had learned that Victoria was her sister. She could imagine her reaction had been less than positive, given they already had a history together, one playing the pauper, the other the princess.

Chelsea checked her phone as it buzzed on top of her covers. Seeing it was her PI, she quickly answered. "This is Chelsea."

Her expression was nothing less than concerned as he informed her that Victoria's sister had just purchased a handgun. When she asked where she was now, he hesitantly admitted he had no idea, she had lost him somewhere after the disturbing purchase. He consoled them both with the fact he had bribed the gun dealer to share her full name and address, triumphantly sharing it with Chelsea now.

He rattled off "Rory Benton, 1000 Fifth Avenue'' before giving the address. He realized she was writing it down and laughed knowing she didn't have a clue. "Save yourself the paper!" he said smugly. He could feel her pause and threw out the big rock. "It's the address of the MET Museum in Manhattan."

Chelsea frowned. "That doesn't make any sense." she said doubtfully.

"It does if you're homeless. And you're a smart ass!" he added.

Chelsea pondered this new piece of information before busting his bubble. "You don't know the half of it. How closely did you look at the photos you took?"

"Close enough. Why do you ask?" he asked cautiously.

"Did you notice she's flipping you off in three of the photos? Somewhere along the way, she made you out!" Chelsea announced none to pleased.

She heard him swear under his breath before answering her, more than a little defensive. "I was discreet, I swear!"

Chelsea cut him some slack. "She's been military trained and served for longer than anyone deserves. It can't be a happy coincidence she bought a gun. Thanks for the heads up."

Disconnecting her phone, she rushed to put on some shoes. She had planned to go tomorrow, not tonight in the middle of a thunderstorm currently pounding all of New York City. But now, knowing Rory was ex-military and had just bought a gun, Chelsea felt a sense of urgency to get to Victoria. Begging her driver to hurry, she could only hope she wouldn't be too late.

THIRTY-NINE

She knocked on the door impatiently, but when no one came to the door, she turned the doorknob for the hell of it, both relieved and concerned that it wasn't locked. Not wanting to startle her, she called out Victoria's name. When there was no answer, she cautiously proceeded to go in search of her. She quickly found her in the family room, a blanket wrapped around her, an open bottle of tequila in front of her, a shot of the clear spirit already poured and waiting.

"Hey Victoria. What's up?" Chelsea asked quietly, going to sit on the cream couch across from the one Victoria occupied.

Victoria took her eyes from the tequila to look at Chelsea. "Why are you in my house? You just don't know when to quit, do you?" Her tone was hostile but surprised to see her there too.

"But you do, don't you Victoria? You remember why you quit? You remember how tequila doesn't work for you?" Ignoring her hostility, Chelsea was doing her damned best to be firm but not poke the bear too hard. "Can I get rid of this for you?"

It was curt, but a nod nonetheless and Chelsea quickly took the tequila to the kitchen to pour it out. She realized Victoria couldn't have drank any of it yet, the shot only poured.

She rejoined Victoria to find she had moved to the end of the couch, more or less in the fetal position. "You didn't answer my question. Why are you in my house?"

Chelsea cut to the chase, seeing no reason not to. "Remember the woman in the picture that I showed you? I'm here to talk about her, about Rory." Realizing Victoria was in a fragile place mentally, Chelsea waited patiently, giving her time to think about what she had said.

She sat up to look at Chelsea, her brow furrowed. "What about Rory? And how do you know her name?"

Chelsea took a deep breath before launching in. "After seeing her in the park I hired a PI to learn more about her. Long story short, she's your sister Victoria. Your twin sister to be exact." She waited for the fallout, not sure how bad it would be.

Victoria looked toward the window as a loud clap of thunder startled them both. "I know." was all she said, her voice quiet.

Chelsea was floored. "You know?" she asked, not able to hide her surprise. "Then you know who your biological mother is too?"

Victoria nodded, swallowing hard before she asked again, her voice now more weary than icy. "Yes, I know. But I still don't know *why* you're in my house?"

Chelsea nodded, moving on to answer her question. "The PI I hired created quite the portofolio on Rory. Did you know she has a short rap sheet from high school? That she served in Iraq after graduation and then was dishonorably discharged from the army? But the real reason I'm here is because she bought a handgun this afternoon and I'm concerned she may come after you. I think she might be holding a grudge against you."

Victoria's laugh was short and bitter. "You think? I got to live in the big house and have two mothers, although to be fair, I didn't know it at the time that they were both my mothers. She, on the other hand, got to live on Staten Island and had to share both her mother *and father* with me, a total spoiled brat who wasn't even smart enough to know how good she had it."

Suddenly a shot rang out and the vase of flowers on the oversized coffee table between them shattered. They instinctively dove for cover, both of them quick to realize Rory must have let herself into the house unannounced.

Neither of them said anything, looking at each other as they crouched behind the couches they had been sitting on seconds ago. "Welcome to my party bitches! Enough with the fun and games. It's time to hunt! Who wants to die first? Bitch one or Bitch two?" Rory asked with an unsettling maniacal laugh.

Seeing Victoria's eyes wide with fear, Chelsea spoke up first. "That seems a little unnecessary, Rory. How about you drop the gun and we can talk and get to know each other better?"

She snorted before answering. "Now who's being unnecessary? Thanks to your PI, we both know you know my story. Torie knows she deserves what's coming to her. And since you had to poke your nose in, now you deserve it too. What else is there left to say?" her voice was icy, her contempt for them both evident.

Suddenly a deafening clap of thunder rattled the house and the lights went out, plunging them all into darkness. The next flash of lightning revealed Victoria trying to make a run for it, yelping out in pain as she was literally shot down, her body making a loud thud as she went down to the floor.

"Thanks for playing Torie! I just grazed your shoulder, a little surface wound-this time. You're welcome. Lucky for you bitches, we have all night and I do have a few things I want to say to you!"

Rory had walked closer to the couches, her lack of fear justified as she was the only one in the room holding a gun. She turned in Chelsea's direction to address her as Chelsea scurried along the back of the couch to the other end.

"You on the other hand, Ms. Logan, I have little to say to so maybe I should hunt you first. You would like that wouldn't you sis, seeing her suffer? After all, she's the one standing between you and your man Alex! Wouldn't you say she should die first?"

Chelsea felt the fear creep in, remembering a similar situation nearly a year ago that also put her life on the line. For a moment she felt paralyzed with fear. Then she shook her head to clear it before she announced with determination, "Not tonight Rory. No one's going to die. You're playing a game you can't win!" While she talked she tried to call 911, discovering she had no service. Frustrated and frantic, she could only assume the storm must be interfering with her reception.

As flashes of lightning lit the dark house here and there, she could see Rory getting closer to her. "I don't think you're in a position to argue." Chelsea ducked as something else shattered not far from her head, Rory's maniacal laugh raising the hairs on her arms. "I'm sure you see my point!"

Concerned about Victoria, Chelsea moved about trying to stay out of sight, but get closer to her. The dark made it easier to move around, but the flashes of lightning were quick to betray you without any warning.

Chelsea finally got herself moved to where she thought Victoria should be, but was alarmed to find a small pool of blood instead. It was easy to see her trail as lightning lit up the floor. Suddenly she realized Rory was behind her. Slowly she turned to look at her. It was like looking at an older, harder Victoria.

"Well, well, hello bitch two. Are you ready to meet your maker? Going up or going down?" She had the gun at her waist, pointed at Chelsea, her maniacal laugh unnerving.

Slowly Chelsea stood up, keeping her hands where she could see them. "Rory, you don't want to do this. So far no crime has been committed. We get why you're pissed off. . ."

She stopped in mid-sentence, noticing Rory's hostile look. "I don't need you to tell me what to do or how to feel. Don't waste your last thoughts on earth on me." She said in short, harsh clips.

Chelsea was desperate, trying to stall for an opportunity to change the narrative that was about to go down. "I'm just saying I understand you. My mom struggled with mental health too. She turned to alcohol to medicate herself. She. . .”

"Shut the hell up! I'm not interested in your interpretation of what your piss poor PI included in the file about me. You don't know squat about me! You are. . ."

Suddenly a body hurtled through the air, tackling Rory and taking her to the ground with a thud. The gun went flying as the two of them struggled on the floor, Chelsea realizing it was Alex. She ran to kick the gun as far away as possible as Rory tried to crawl her way to it, Alex sitting on top of her and trying to contain her. Chelsea grabbed a heavy vase on a nearby table and raised it over her head, coming down hard on Rory's head. She dropped like a hot potato, no one there to catch her.

They both stood there, breathing hard at the exertion of it all. Cautiously Alex picked himself up off of her. He gave her a nudge with his foot, checking to make sure she was out. Chelsea watched as he took off his belt and used it to tie her hands behind her back. When he finally looked at her, he could see she was close to tears. Quickly he moved beside her, pulling her into a tight hug.

"I thought I was going to die, Alex! I thought that bitch was going to kill me, but all I could think about was wanting to tell you one more time I love you! If you hadn't got here when. . . "

He was shushing her, stroking her head. "You're safe, I've got you and I'm never going to let you go." His voice emotional too, "If I would have lost you Chelsea!" he said, burying his head in her shoulder.

They both jumped at the sound of a moan. They looked at Rory to make sure it wasn't her. Then Chelsea started to look around frantically. "It's Victoria. Rory shot her earlier!" she said, running to where she had found the blood earlier. They found her in a heap, conscious but bleeding profusely from her wound. They blinked as the lights suddenly came on and they could see the mess of what had gone down.

Alex had his phone out dialing 911, handing it to Chelsea as he bent down to tend to Victoria. "Watch the girl!" he demanded.

As Chelsea gave the dispatcher the address for Victoria's home, she turned her attention back to Rory. She gasped to discover she was gone.

FORTY

The chaos of the scene looked like it was an episode out of Castle, only thankfully there were no dead bodies. As the paramedics loaded Victoria onto the stretcher, Alex had gone to get a blanket and wrap it around Chelsea. He held her to him tightly as they both watched them load Victoria into the ambulance.

She could hear the regret in his voice. "I have to go with her. You understand that right?'

She nodded numbly as he opened the door of the car, kissing the top of her head before she climbed into it. "I'll be there as soon as I can." he said to Chelsea before turning to Kenny, the driver. "I need you to walk her up to her apartment and please double check it before you leave." he told him.

Chelsea knew Kenny was a long trusted driver and they both knew he would take good care of her until Alex could be there. It killed him to send her off without him, but what could he do? Victoria had been shot and needed him having no one else to be with her except for him. He felt bad for Victoria, all she was going through, the latest on the list having been shot. The hardest part of it all though, was where the hell had Rory disappeared to? When and where would she resurface? And would they be so lucky the next time?

It was well after midnight and Chelsea was in bed, her small lamp beside the bed, the only light on in her bedroom. She was exhausted both emotionally and physically, but lay in the king size bed wide awake. She was in a mental debate with herself, arguing when and if Alex would actually show. It made her heart ache to know this would always be their reality, Victoria needing Alex and him going to her every time. It was why she had made her Paris plan to begin with, finding it the best way for her to bow out gracefully.

She picked up the book on her bedside table and found her glasses. It was the best way to distract herself and maybe even get some sleep. She found herself rereading paragraphs, knowing she didn't have a clue what was happening between the pages. She kept reading though and eventually nodded off, not even knowing when Alex came in.

He stood at her doorway, watching her sleep. He had not stopped thinking about her as he filled out paperwork for Victoria, checked in with her doctor, and eventually sat by her bedside until her drugs kicked in and she fell asleep. Her shoulder wound was a little more than superficial, but she had lost a lot of blood and they had agreed to keep her overnight. Sooner or later he would have to deal with what going home would look like for her. For now, he couldn't wait to crawl into bed with Chelsea and hold her to him.

He moved quietly as he undressed and then pulled the covers back to join her. He smiled when he saw she was sleeping in one of his old t-shirts. She always said it was one of her favorites, telling him how soft it was and that it always smelled like him, even after being freshly washed.

She jumped when he touched her, but quickly relaxed seeing it was him and gladly let him pull her to him.

At first he just held her until eventually he pulled her face up to look at him before kissing her ever so gently. "You know how much I love you right? I'm so sorry I wasn't there for you tonight."

Chelsea tilted her head back to look at him better. "But you were there for me tonight. I wouldn't be here if you hadn't saved me tonight. Both of us were lucky you showed up when you did. And I do know you love me. I love you too."

He kissed her again, a soft kiss at first, one arm keeping her close, his free hand holding her face next to his. As his kiss deepened and became more urgent, he could feel Chelsea's body responding, her leg going over his and pulling herself even closer to him.

"I know it's late, but right now I need to feel every inch of you in every way, inside and out. If that's okay with you?" His voice was husky, his emotions running too deep to bother hiding.

She nodded her agreement before simply whispering, "yes." She held her arms up over her head as he slid the t-shirt off. True to his word, his lips found every inch of her, taking his time, so gentle but sexy as hell at the same time. She could feel his controlled strength and soaked it all up, letting him soothe away some of the night's trauma. She had been waiting and needing that from him and realized he was desperate to give it to her as well.

It had been two weeks since they had been together and she had missed the feel of him in more ways than one. It was the wee hours of the morning before they finally seemed to have satisfied their needs. Chelsea rolled away from him to get out of bed and retrieve her t-shirt and panties he had thrown to the floor earlier.

He sat up half way and asked, "Hey, where you going?" as she opened the bedroom door.

She turned back to him sheepishly. "I just want to make sure the doors are locked."

He nodded, understanding her worries were more than warranted.

She didn't turn any lights on but walked to the door in her bare feet, checking each of the locks first. Then she turned to the bar and picked up one of the heavy barstools and put it in front of the door. She knew she was being silly, but it made her feel better anyway.

As she went to the kitchen for a drink of water, she realized someone was sitting on her couch. Rory smiled wickedly, giving her a little wave. "Aren't you going to put one in front of your sliding door too? Oops, too late!"

"How the hell did you get in here?" Chelsea asked, trying to keep her voice steady.

"Does it matter? You had to know we have unfinished business." She got up and walked towards her, her eyes looking her over from head to toe. As Chelsea started to scream for Alex, Rory put her finger to her lips and shook her head. "Don't do it or you'll regret it."

Chelsea thought of all the rage she had ever had for all the shit ever dumped on her. This bitch was not going to be the one to take her down. With all her might she swung her fist up and punched Rory in the face as hard as she could. She was shocked to see her fall to the ground. Quickly she made a mad dash for her bedroom, rushing to close the door and lock it.

Alex sat up in bed, his look first confused and then concerned. "What?" he asked.

"She's out there. I went to lock the doors and when I turned around, she was sitting on the couch!" Chelsea was borderline hysterical and Alex quickly went to her. "I punched her in the face as hard as I could and she went down."

Alex grabbed his phone and dialed 911. He stood beside her at the door, neither of them sure what to do. Quietly he spoke into his phone giving her address and the situation at hand. Chelsea could feel his fury as he turned to her and asked if she were hurt. She looked at her throbbing knuckles but shook her head no.

She continued to stand between him and the door, her hand on his chest, terrified he would want to go out there. Their eyes locked on each other as they heard things crashing about, but neither of them ventured out. They could hear sirens and suddenly the apartment was quiet. Cautiously they opened her door, finding the living room empty, the sliding glass door open, her drapes billowing slightly in the breeze. Chelsea looked around, the damage Rory had inflicted in a mere minute or two appalling.

For the second time that night, they found themselves in the middle of a crime scene. They watched from the couch as officers took notes and made observations around her apartment. At one point an officer stood up and announced, "There's fresh blood here."

Chelsea looked mortified momentarily before realizing it must be from the punch she had thrown at Rory's face. She had neglected to share that part when telling her story of what had happened and once again they made her run it from the top.

Finally, everyone was gone and the apartment was theirs again. Exhausted they climbed into bed after Chelsea double checked all the locks and put her bedroom chair in front of her door. It was a bitter pill to swallow, but when all was said and done, there was little they could say or do. For now, Rory was winning.

For now.

FORTY-ONE

I t had been a couple of days since Rory had come into Victoria's home and wreaked havoc in their lives. Chelsea was at Hudon & Butler, trying hard to let work distract her. As the intercom on her desk buzzed, she answered it, still focused on what she was doing.

"This is Chelsea." she said after picking up.

"It's Victoria. I'm sorry to disturb your day, but I wondered if I could have a conversation with you?" her voice was subdued and respectful. Alex had told her the doctors said her wound should heal nicely, but mentally she still seemed fragile. They all walked on eggshells knowing Rory was still out there and her next move unpredictable.

Alex was working overtime to keep them both safe, having hired extra security for the building and personal bodyguards for both Victoria and Chelsea. Now she hesitated only briefly before agreeing to indulge Victoria in her request.

"Of course Victoria. Where would you like me to meet you?" She said, keeping her tone light.

"I'll need you for the afternoon. I was hoping you would go with me to my house. You and our entourage of course." she said.

Chelsea hesitated. Rory holding the gun on her flashed before her eyes. She wasn't sure she was up for Victoria's request. Sensing her hesitation, Victoria added softly, "Please Chelsea? You're the only one who understands how difficult this is. You may be even better than me. I'd consider it a personal favor. There's much for us to talk about on the ride to Brooklyn as well."

It was hard to trust her, but Chelsea agreed to meet her downstairs in an hour. As she got ready to disconnect she heard Victoria add one more request. "Alex doesn't need to come. This is between me and you."

Chelsea sat in her chair trying to sooth her misgivings. She hadn't seen Victoria since the incident, respecting the space she assumed she needed. She was staying at Alex's apartment again, but he had assured Chelsea it was temporary and that she should stay there too. He argued it would be easier if they were all under one roof. She had declined, knowing it would only be easier for Alex and nothing but awkward for the women.

Now she got up to go see Alex and see what his thoughts were on Victoria's request. The secretary ushered her right in and she smiled to see him bent over his work at his desk, shirt sleeves rolled up, his eyes big behind his glasses. It seemed so normal and Chelsea embraced the moment regardless of how fleeting the feeling was.

When he saw her, he got up and immediately came to her. "What's up? Is everything okay?" he asked cautiously.

"You tell me. Victoria just called me and asked me to join her in riding out to Brooklyn in an hour. She said we have some things to discuss and not to bother you, that the conversation is just between us girls." Chelsea announced watching his face for a reaction.

Alex nodded, sitting back on the edge of his desk, crossing his arms in front of him. "She's going home today. We had a long heart to heart this morning over our coffee."

"How lovely for the two of you." she responded, trying not to sound sarcastic about it.

He frowned. "After all you two have been through together, you still don't trust her?" he sounded a little surprised which irritated Chelsea even just a little bit more.

"What's changed that indicates I can trust her? Because she got shot? Or because you two were all cozy this morning?" she asked.

Alex went to her, putting his hands on her shoulders. "I'm going to tell you the same thing I told her this morning. I care about her and I want to be there for her, but" As Chelsea tried to pull away, he held her in place. "BUT I'm in love with you. She is my past and you're for the rest of my life and she is going to have to accept that or." He paused, "Or we're going to need to part ways. So I'm hopeful she wants to try and work it out."

Chelsea stared him down, thinking over the words he was telling her. She had heard it before and yet, Victoria seemed to always come in first. She was skeptical they could find a way.

Alex seemed to know what she was thinking. "I promise you Chelsea, I love you and you're my first priority from now on. Victoria and I both know she loves to embrace the drama, but she's going to have to start doing it without including me. The only girl I'm here for is you, whether you're flying high or falling hard, I'm going to be here for you." He pulled her in for a kiss, his lips and tongue trying their damndest to prove his point as he went long and deep, his hands on either side of her face.

Wanting to believe him, she kissed him back, reluctant to let him go. He might be convinced and Victoria might have said all the right things this morning, but she was doubtful their thruple woes were over.

On top of that there were some serious loose ends hanging over the three of them, the biggest one being where in the hell was Rory? Would she surface tomorrow during Victoria's father's funeral? Or would they keep walking on eggshells waiting for her to make good on her promises? Feeling uneasy, Chelsea went to get her bag and head downstairs to meet Victoria and her car. For Alex's sake, she would play nice, but she would also keep her guard up. Clearly, one of them needed to.

FORTY-TWO

They sat in silence the first ten minutes or so, Chelsea waiting for Victoria to go first and Victoria seemingly hesitant to do so. Chelsea pulled her water bottle out of her bag, needing something to keep her hands busy. She had some serious anxiety about returning to the scene of the crime, the gun pointed at her still a vivid memory.

"It's hard to go back, isn't it?" Victoria asked, her voice sad.

"Actually it really is. I keep seeing Rory pointing her gun at me and believing I was going to die." Chelsea couldn't help but be honest.

"I wanted to thank you for that night Chelsea. You were so brave. I went to run and you stood up to her, for both of us. Thank you for that. Alex told me about you hitting her over the head with one of my vases. That took guts." Victoria was looking at her, her tone sincere.

Chelsea nodded. "It was more instinct than anything. I'm not very good at backing down when my back's against the wall. It's gotten me into trouble a time or two."

Victoria laughed softly. "I can imagine. You've been taking care of yourself for a long time haven't you? You deserve to be happy with someone like Alex."

Chelsea arched her brow at Victoria. "Like Alex? Or actually with Alex?" She tried to keep the sarcasm out of her voice, hearing Alex in her head telling her again not to poke the bear.

"Touché!" Victoria responded. She turned back to the window, seeming to be lost in thought. Abruptly she turned back to Chelsea.

"He loves you, you know. He lights up when he talks about you. He tells me you're his future, his forever person."

Chelsea wasn't sure if she heard regret or sadness in her voice, but there was no hostility and she took that as a step in the right direction for both of them. She decided to take the high road.

"I appreciate you saying that. I know he loves you too and will always care about your well being." Even as she said it, she cringed realizing how much that must suck to hear her words.

She heard Victoria give a clipped laugh. "Friends, not to be confused with lovers. I got his memo, no worries."

"You know he's hoping *we* can become friends?" Chelsea added.

Victoria laughed for real this time. "He always sees the good in people, such an optimist. He can't help it, he gets it from his mother, the therapist, always helping people be the best versions of themselves."

Chelsea tucked that nugget away and played along. "I told him a while back he seems to have a type."

Victoria rolled her eyes. "What? Bitch on wheels?" She was smiling as she said it, Chelsea not offended in the least.

"I've been called worse." she said with a smile of her own.

"Haven't we all darling, haven't we all!" Victoria's expression changed suddenly as her house came into view. Chelsea could feel her anxiety and her own as well. Alex had instructed the bodyguard to go in first and make sure everything was clear before the women did.

They sat quietly in the car, both of them stuck in their own thoughts. Victoria got out of the car as a woman walked to it. Realizing it was her housekeeper, Chelsea got out of the car too. As the trunk popped open, she realized Victoria was retrieving her overnight bag to carry into the house.

"Wait! Are you really staying here tonight?" she asked Victoria.

"It's time. I can't live my life in fear. What would be the point in that?" she asked somberly. Noticing their bodyguard was giving them an all clear signal, the three women walked into the house.

The housekeeper headed to Victoria's bedroom after taking her bag from her while the guard announced he would be right outside should they need him for anything. The two women looked at each other before Chelsea followed Victoria into her family room.

The afternoon sunlight streaming through the windows made the room seem warm and friendly, a far cry from that stormy night. Chelsea looked around the room, any sign of a disturbance wiped clean. Even the shattered vase that sat on the glass coffee table had been replaced with a replica, currently graced with fresh cream colored roses. She watched as Victoria bent over to smell them before taking a seat.

Victoria waved her hand, indicating Chelsea should join her on the other couch. "I wanted to talk to you about a few things Chelsea." she said quietly.

Her old instincts kicked in, but she sat down anyway asking somewhat apprehensively. "About what?"

"First, I'm not going to publish the book. I appreciate all your efforts to make the possibility a reality, but now things are different and I've changed my mind." Her eyes were steady on Chelsea, almost like she expected an argument about it.

"I get that and understand." Chelsea said, relieved their conversation was business related.

"However," Victoria paused dramatically as Chelsea tried not to wince, mentally preparing herself for the other shoe to fall. "I loved your idea of hosting a fundraiser for the Susan G. Komen Foundation. I think it's important to create an opportunity to educate women about breast cancer and the importance of early detection. Technically we would create a philanthropic event with Hudson & Butler, but it would be hosted in memory of my mother. When the time comes, I would love to have your help with this. If you're up for it?"

Chelsea was relieved, happy to hear Victoria embrace her idea. With or without the book, it was a much healthier and productive opportunity to mark the loss of her mother. "I would love to help you with your event. I assume you would want to schedule it for sometime in October, since it is recognized as Breast Cancer Awareness Month?"

Victoria nodded before answering. "Of course. We will need to hustle to make it happen this year, but it's the perfect distraction I need in my life right now. Thank you for the idea and for agreeing to help me. Now for the next item of business."

Again, Chelsea worked hard to keep her expression neutral. "I love your Paris idea. I believe it's a great way to bring international authors into Hudson & Butler. And if we're going to have another office, Paris is the perfect place to open one."

There it was. Chelsea had not presented opening another office as that would be a bigger commitment and could quite possibly relocate her permanently to Paris. It was one thing to go for six to seven weeks, but she was not interested in a new address. She didn't have to hear Alex in her head to know to tread lightly.

"Tell me more about that Victoria. What exactly are you thinking?" she asked, keeping her voice even keel. She crossed her fingers that Victoria wanted to be the one to go there.

She was relishing in this moment a little too much as she said to Chelsea. "I'm thinking you came up with a productive way to get your-self to Paris, all expenses paid and now I'm prepared to hand it to you on a silver platter. I'm thinking you're a smart girl and know a golden opportunity when you see one. I'm thinking we need an office in Paris and you're perfect for it!"

Chelsea could feel her heart starting to pound. Was this bitch really trying to make her choose between Alex and Paris? It was hands down an easy decision.

"If Hudson & Butler is interested in sponsoring a writer's retreat in Paris, I am more than happy to spearhead that event. In my proposal I outlined the agenda for the six week retreat including a budget, recruit-ing prospective authors, and what my role would be as the editor on sight. As for opening and managing a permanent office in Paris, I would decline that." She waited for the chips to fall,

Victoria cocked her head to one side, her look intense. "Not even if the price is right? Obviously we value and trust you here and even more there so it seems only fair to let you name your price for such a commitment. What would it take to put you in an apartment in Paris, say for a one year contract?"

Chelsea could feel the heat start to rise. She should have known Victoria was still trying to get rid of her. Well two could play her game. "Really? For one year, I would need a million dollars and all expenses paid. For that, I might think about it."

"Done!" said Victoria, her look triumphant.

FORTY-THREE

On a whim Chelsea had thrown out the biggest number she could imagine, well beyond her current salary, a number she never imagined Victoria would accept. Now she sat there, her look smug, her hand stretched out to her to shake on their deal. Chelsea should have known better than to play with fire.

She stood up abruptly, her look feigning disappointment. "Just when I thought we were going to be book besties, you make a bitch move like that one." Chelsea picked up her bag before turning back for one last parting shot.

"You don't have enough money in the world for me to relocate and leave Alex. You said it yourself, I'm his future. Forget the writer's retreat, I don't need Paris." She headed for the door only to be halted by Victoria's next statement.

"Really? So it's true? Your relationship is so fragile it can't handle one year of long distance? And honestly Chelsea, I thought you were more business savvy than that. Can you really afford to turn down a million dollars over a *man*?"

Chelsea paused to turn back to Victoria. "I'm not going to take your bait. If you're not interested in the writer's retreat project, then let it go. And you can send me away for a year or a million years, but I will always be his forever person." She turned again to walk out, trying not to show how rattled she was by Victoria's bullshit.

"Fine. Then you're fired." Victoria was standing now too, her hands on her hips as Chelsea turned back to her once again.

"What did you just say?" she asked incredulously.

"You heard me. If you don't want this opportunity to grow both yourself and Hudson & Butler, with this very generous offer I might add, then you're fired."

Chelsea snorted, "You can't do that! Alex would never sign off on that!"

Victoria's laugh was condescending to say the least. "Maybe you're not aware, but what happens at Hudson & Butler is not a fifty-fifty split. The by-laws are written to protect my financial investment to its fullest and even Alex bows down to my final decisions. You can ask him yourself."

Chelsea walked back over to Victoria wanting nothing more than to slap the smug look off her face. "You'll regret messing with this bitch if you don't rethink your bullshit." She turned on her heel to stalk out. She was just at the door when Victoria shot back.

"Fine! I'll make it for two million! Best and final offer. One year."

Chelsea turned to look back at Victoria, her face impossible to read. "Put it in writing." was all she said before she finally walked out for real.

Chelsea sat in the car, fuming over just how she was going to handle Paris now. She was mentally kicking herself for letting her guard down. Victoria had worked her charm, making them feel connected, making her feel they were on the same page. Clearly she should have known better. How could she have been so stupid? She was losing her bitchy ways and she blamed Alex for that. Which brought her to her next concern. How much was she going to tell Alex? How would he take it?

Clearly Victoria was desperate to have her gone, and she was still shocked to hear her throw out her final offer. She was curious how much truth there was to her having the final say, but she did recall a time Alex had warned her not to push so hard as to jeopardize everything he had worked for at Hudson & Butler Publishing.

A part of her did question if she was crazy to turn down such an extravagant salary as well as a year living in Paris, even for Alex. He hadn't seemed happy about her short version, what would he have to say about the long version. If they were truly soulmates, their relationship should be able to survive a year on different continents. Right?

She hated being in this position and would literally love to kick Victoria's butt from New York to Paris. Clearly she had cornered Chelsea into putting a price tag on her relationship with Alex. What she hated most was knowing Victoria made some good points. Was she gutsy enough to find out if their relationship really was so fragile it would not survive a year apart? More importantly, who was she to turn down two million dollars?

FORTY-FOUR

She had been back in Manhattan long enough to check-in with Alex and go for a long run through Central Park. She had a lot to think about and a run always helped get her thoughts in order. Now as she showered, she was somewhat discouraged that her plan was feeble at best, relying on her old Chelsea ways. Chelsea considered she was dealing with a ticking time bomb and as such would need to handle it with the utmost care, particularly as her track record was not great.

She dressed in one of her dresses she knew Alex could not resist her in. She ordered his favorite pasta to be delivered and found a bottle of wine to chill. It was a gorgeous day and would be a perfect evening to have dinner on their apartment terrace. She was pulling out all the stops knowing Alex was already having a hard day.

When she talked to him earlier, he reminded her he was giving Victoria's father's eulogy tomorrow during the afternoon service and wanted to finish it up before he headed home. She could imagine how hard that must be, noticing how tired he sounded over the phone. Her phone buzzed as he let her know he was a few minutes away. It was go time.

She greeted him at the door, kissing him lightly on the cheek as she took his briefcase. Together they headed to the bar, two glasses of wine already poured. She had the pasta staying warm in the oven and went to pull it out, announcing proudly, "I cooked tonight!"

He laughed as she hoped he would before saying, "Good! I'm starving. I can't remember if I even ate today." It was then he noticed the open sliding door. He took his glass of wine with him and went to investigate.

"This looks nice." was all he said as she went to join him. He took in the large candles lit around the furniture strategically placed around the gas fire pit. It looked cozy and just what he needed.

She laid her head on his shoulder, her hand through his arm. "It's such a beautiful night and I thought we could both use some fresh air"

He put his arm around her and kissed the top of her head. "I definitely need a change of scenery. And a big plate of pasta!"

Chelsea nodded before answering, "Coming right up. Have a seat and relax."

They had worked their way through dinner and almost finished a bottle of wine, the music playing on the bluetooth speaker. Chelsea regretted there was so much hanging over both of them, wishing they could just enjoy each other on such a beautiful night. She punted her plan, not sure if she was chickening out or being smart about when to execute it.

Alex's arm was around her as they sat close together watching the flames dance before them. "So, what gives?" he asked in her ear, his breath warm on her neck.

She turned to look at him. "What do you mean?"

He laughed softly. "I know when I'm being played. Wine, my favorite pasta, the dress that drives me crazy. You want something or you have something to tell me."

Damn! Alex always could see right through her. She turned to him. "You're right, I do."

"I assume it has something to do with your conversation with Victoria today?" She could see him bracing himself.

She crawled into his lap, pressing herself against him. "What I want is you Alex. I want you to take me to bed and let me have my way with you. Does that work for you?"

He smiled at her, his eyes dark. "Fine. We can play it your way. What do you have in mind?"

She went to turn off the gas on the fire pit and blow out the candles before she came back to him, straddling him on the outdoor couch. She took possession of his mouth, her tongue deep inside, leaving no doubt what she had in mind.

"I think we should move this party for two inside." she said as she moved to his neck and nibbled his ear.

He picked her up and carried her inside with her legs wrapped around him. He sat her down in the middle of the living room, but headed her in the direction of the bedroom before saying, "I'll be there in a minute. Just going to lock up."

She smiled back at him. "Don't be long." she said as she let her dress drop to the floor, walking out of it as she went to the bedroom.

Quickly he checked all the locks as promised before heading to the bedroom, undressing as he went. He knew something was up with Chelsea, but he wasn't against taking the long way to get there. In fact, he enjoyed taking the long way and would happily let her have her way with him all night long.

It was getting late and Chelsea was enjoying Alex's arms around her, feeling loved and safe. Having abandoned her plan, she was relishing in their night together just the two of them, knowing the chaos that tomorrow could bring. But Alex wasn't going to let her off that easily.

"Alright, it's time to spill. What happened with you and Victoria today?" he asked.

Chelsea winced mentally, having assumed he would let it go. She should have known better. She turned to face him, keeping her expression neutral, her voice light. "First, she let me know she's not going to publish the book." She paused, giving him time to respond.

"That's good news right? It would be in really poor taste to pursue that now." He was looking cautiously hopeful. "What else?"

Chelsea nodded. "Also she loved my idea of hosting a fundraiser for Susan G. Komen and asked me to help her with that, which of course I said yes to."

He looked at her, his gaze steady. "We talked about how you want us to be friends and she mentioned you can't help yourself because you get it from your mother. She's a school counselor, right?"

"You already know that. Stop stalling and get to the point." He said, getting impatient.

She took a deep breath. "It's about Paris. She wants to open an office there for Hudson & Butler and she wants me to be the one to do it. For a million dollars and a one year contract."

Eyes narrowed, Alex asked the inevitable. "What the hell? What did you say to that?"

"I laughed in her face. Then she accused me of being a fool instead of a business woman and having no faith in our relationship if we can't handle dating long distance for one year." She held her breath, watching his reaction closely.

He rolled over to his back, his arm across the top of his head. "You two really don't know when to quit, do you?"

"Me? I just wanted to run a writer's retreat and give you two some space to get your selves back in check. She's the crazy one!" Chelsea could feel the heat rising and not the kind she had enjoyed less than an hour ago.

"Let me guess. She didn't accept your rejection of her offer?" Alex asked, his voice hard.

Chelsea shook her head miserably. "She said she would fire me if I didn't take it. When I still refused, she offered me two million dollars to go for one year."

She heard Alex's sharp breath, his shock evident. He was silent, clearly processing what Chelsea had just shared with him.

"You know I wouldn't let her fire you, right?" he finally asked.

Chelsea was hesitant to tell him the rest of it. "She said she's the bottom line and it wouldn't matter what you would want to do."

"Damn her!" Alex exclaimed. He got out of bed and grabbed his navy robe off the chair. "I need some air" was all he said before opening the bedroom door.

Chelsea found her robe too and went to join him on their terrace. She came up behind him, putting her arms around his waist and laying her head on his back. "I told her if she wasn't interested in my six week writer's retreat, I don't want Paris."

He pulled away from her and turned to look at her. "But you do want it, don't you? Not just the retreat, but the new office and the two million dollars."

FORTY-FIVE

She had tried to deny it, but he refused to believe her and after a while she had to admit it was a hard offer to resist, especially if getting fired was the alternative. They talked in circles around it before finally agreeing to let it go for the night.

They had gone back to bed on a much more somber note, but she knew he was awake in the dark, just as she lay there pretending to sleep as well. Her practical side was telling her she would be a fool to decline such an offer, but the emotional side of her insisted there was no way in hell she was leaving Alex for a year. It was going to be a long night followed by a long day tomorrow.

At five am Alex rolled out of bed for his morning workout before showering promptly at six. As she loved to do, she got out of bed and went to join him.

She knocked on the door, the formality of it causing her to wonder if she should just give him space. She loved to see him naked and sudsy in the shower, his dark wet hair unruly as always.

"Can I join you? Or are you busy planning out your day?" she asked, trying to sound casual.

He smiled at her before asking, "What took you so long?"

Despite last night's tension, they easily fell into their shower habits. Too soon they were toweling off and moving onto starting their day. They had their work bags, juices, and coffee, when there was a knock on the door. Alex opened it cautiously, discovering it was a delivery. He looked at the name scrawled across it before handing it to Chelsea.

She could recognize Victoria's handwriting anywhere and immediately assumed it was the contract Chelsea had asked her to put in writing. She left it unopened and tossed it casually on the bartop before rejoining Alex, ready to head out the door. She waited for him to open it, but instead he turned to her, setting her bag and coffee down before pulling her into his arms.

"What is it Alex?" she asked him worriedly.

His look was warm but serious. "Before we leave I need you to know I realize this could be a big opportunity for you despite the motivation behind Victoria's offer. Victoria does not have the power here, you do because it's your decision and I will support you either way. Either way, you will not be fired because she and I both know you're the breath of fresh air Hudson & Butler desperately needed. Most importantly Chelsea, I'm here for you and I love you more than you can imagine. It would be hard to be so far away from you, but a year apart will not make or break our relationship. I'm not going anywhere. I love you!" He pulled her to him, holding her tightly.

She could hear the emotion in his voice and felt her own emotions stirring. She buried her face in his shoulder, wishing he would never let her go.

She looked up at him, her expression a mixture of relief and appreciation. "That means so much to me for you to say that. You mean the world to me Alex and I don't want to risk losing you. I love you so much. You're right, it could be a tremendous opportunity for me professionally, but a year can be a long time. And I don't even know if I'm ready for so much responsibility. I don't know what to do. It would be easier if you just asked me not to go!" She said woefully.

He laughed out loud. "Yeah right! I'm pretty sure you were born ready! And sorry, it's all on you, but I will support and love you no matter what you decide. If you decide to go, we'll figure it out." He kissed her long and deep before saying in her ear, "I love you Chelsea, today and always."

She held onto him tightly, not wanting to ever let him go. How would she possibly survive without him for a year? Releasing her, he handed her bag and coffee back to her, before ushering her out the door.

They were quiet as they made the short ride to Hudson & Butler, both of them deep in thought. Was she really ready to run an office on her own? She glanced at Alex, his face tired. She suddenly remembered he had other things to worry about than just her going to Paris. He had an eulogy to give this afternoon and she knew they both just needed to get through this funeral. Rory was still on the loose, and today seemed like an opportunity she would be unable to resist.

When his eyes met hers, he seemed to read her mind. "Stay alert today. She is bound to show up. I will have men everywhere, but stay alert." He said softly, squeezing her hand before leaning over to kiss her on the cheek. She closed her eyes, inhaling the smell of him.

She knew he was worried about her and Victoria, but she worried about the toll this was taking on him, on both of them. She knew he felt a tremendous responsibility to keep them both safe. She picked up his hand and kissed it. "I promise, but you promise me you'll stay alert too."

He smiled reassuringly at her. "Nothings going to happen to me. But I'll be alert, I promise."

They had agreed Alex should get there at least an hour before the funeral to be there for Victoria. She had questioned if she even needed to be there, but he had insisted she did and she agreed to arrive later, her presence discreet and primarily there to support Alex. And keep an eye out for Rory.

It was still early when she arrived and she immediately went in search of Alex and Victoria. She found Victoria at the front of the sanctuary rearranging a plethora of flowers around her father's casket. Seeing her, Victoria immediately walked over.

"Victoria. Is there anything I can do to help you?" she asked, her voice respectful and somber.

"Yes! Can you tell me where the hell Alex is? He was supposed to be here thirty minutes ago! I need him here!" Victoria's voice was shrill, her emotions clearly running high.

Chelsea answered her calmly. "I know he left before I did, I'm sure he's here somewhere. I'll go find him for you."

Victoria looked relieved and actually thanked her before turning back to the floral arrangements. Chelsea hurried off, assuming Alex had run into people he knew. The least she could do for Victoria today was to deliver him as promised.

Twenty minutes later she had searched everywhere with no luck. Feeling a little frantic, she called the car service to see if they were stuck in traffic but no one answered. She hated like hell to go back and tell

Victoria Alex wasn't there yet. More importantly, she worried where he could possibly be.

As she walked up behind Victoria, Chelsea could tell she was clearly agitated as she spoke with an older woman. As she got a closer look, she realized it was the housekeeper Victoria had grown up with, her biological mother. She could immediately see the resemblance between the two women. Seeing the seriousness of their conversation, Chelsea gently put a hand on each of them, guiding them into a small room off of the sanctuary, away from prying eyes.

"I don't know why you're here! You're not invited to my father's funeral!" Victoria was saying, her face mad as hell.

"You won't answer my calls, so I came today. I have a few things to say to you and you're going to listen!"

"I do not have time for this! You need to go!" Victoria said, her hostility apparent.

The woman pointed to a chair and demanded "Sit down!" When she hesitated she added firmly, "Now Torie!" Chelsea watched in amazement as Victoria did as she was told.

"I know you were devastated to lose your mother. She loved you more than anything in the world, but making her deathbed confession to you the way she did was not okay. She was not a strong woman and when your father brought you to her, she didn't ask any questions. She didn't know that her husband was actually your father. She didn't know that her housekeeper was actually your mother, or even that you were a twin. She only knew she was overjoyed to hold you in her arms, to love you, to watch you grow, and take care of you the best she could."

Chelsea watched as Victoria let silent tears slide down her face, looking down at her hands, listening but not able to look at her biological mother. The woman handed her a tissue from her purse before she continued.

"Your father and I fell in love. We did not intend to, it just happened. He would get home so late and your mother would already be in bed, her sleeping pill having kicked in long ago. He would be hungry and needing someone to talk to about his day. At first we were just friends, then we were friends that drank wine together over dinner, then we fell in love. He needed someone to take care of him just like he tried to take care of your mother. He worked so hard to give your mother everything she wanted, and yet she rarely seemed to be happy. Until she got pregnant. She was glowing from the minute she knew."

She took a deep breath before she continued. "They were both so happy. A week after they shared their news, I was stunned to find out I was also pregnant. I was scared and I didn't share my news until I was showing and forced too. When your father found out, he promised to take care of the baby and me. When we found out we were having twins, we were stunned together. Then the unthinkable happened when their baby died, just a week old. Your mother could not handle her loss and your father worried she would not survive it. It was my idea to give you to them." She paused to look at Victoria, putting her hand up to caress her face.

"My sweet beautiful baby girl. Your father refused at first, the thought incomprehensible. He worried about what people would say, but adoption was an easy story to tell. Your mother was so fragile, but you were always her ray of sunshine."

Victoria was all but sobbing now, nodding her head sadly. "I know. I felt that even when I was young. She was depressed so often, but never showed it when I was around. I knew something wasn't right but I assumed it was because my father was never home. Work was a poor excuse when a little girl just wanted one of her parents to read her a bedtime story! But you, you were always there for me. I always told my friends you were like my second mother." A sob escaped her as she said it.

"Because I was your second mother. I am still Torie! I love you and I want you to let me back into your life. You need me as much as I need you!" Now they were both crying and Chelsea felt awkward watching the emotional display between them.

Suddenly Victoria shook her head, her demeanor changing in an instant. "Just one thing mother dearest. What will Rory have to say about that? She seems to have a lot of anger and who can blame her? While you were putting me to bed, who was putting her to bed? Not her mother or her father. She hates me!" Victoria had flipped the narrative just like that.

It was her mother's turn to nod her head in agreement. "I know. I failed her miserably and she is still paying the price." The woman pulled another tissue from her purse to wipe her own eyes. Chelsea noticed something fall out as she pulled her tissue out and bent over to retrieve it, handing it to the woman.

She handed the folded piece of paper to Victoria worriedly. "I forgot I had this! Rory gave this to me late last night and asked me to give it to you today, knowing I was coming to the funeral."

She took it from her mother, opening it suspiciously. She was quick to read it before looking at Chelsea in alarm.

"What is it?" Chelsea asked with concern. Victoria handed it to her before starting to pace around the room.

"It's about Alex! She has him and wants us to come. But she didn't give an address. It just says you know where I am!" Victoria was incredulous. "How would we know where she is?"

Chelsea read it through twice, a pit starting to form in her stomach. Her face was grim as she announced, "I know where she is! It's not that far, but we need to go and we need to go now!"

"Now? Now! I have a funeral happening in thirty minutes! How am I supposed to leave now?" Victoria was bordering on hysterical. "My sister is a lunatic!" she shouted.

They both looked at Victoria, surprised to hear her refer to Rory as her sister, the familiarity of using the term sister not lost on either of them.

Chelsea shook her head. "The note says we both need to come if we ever want to see Alex again! And to come alone! Are you coming or not?"

Victoria announced, "Fine! I'll go with you!" She then turned to her mother. "Can you please let everyone know there will be a thirty minute delay? But we *are* having this funeral today if it kills me!" Chelsea shuddered, thinking to herself, careful what you throw to the universe Victoria.

FORTY-SEVEN

S he flagged down her car and both of them climbed into the back seat. Chelsea still had the note in her hand, leaning forward to tell the driver "The Met Museum, but please go to the back, the kitchen door."

Victoria looked at her, shaking her head. "How could you possibly know that's where she is?"

Chelsea showed her the note, reading it to her. 'Meet me at the back unless you want Alex served up cold. You know the address.' Seeing her puzzled look, she explained further.

"When my PI was following Rory, she gave the address of the Met Museum to the gun dealer. My guess is she's homeless some of the time. The Met has a kitchen they serve food from. That has to be where she and Alex are." Chelsea was convincing and Victoria chose to believe her.

They watched out their windows, each of them anxious to get there. Victoria was the first to say it. "What's our plan when we get there? We just pop into the kitchen and exchange Alex for what? Does she still want me dead? You gave her a black eye. Does she want you dead too?"

Chelsea looked at Victoria in surprise. She didn't remember telling her she had punched Rory in the face that night nor did she even know if she had given her a black eye. Something wasn't adding up. Chelsea started to dig in her bag, looking for anything that might be used as a weapon but found nothing.

As the driver came to a stop, Chelsea tried to keep her voice light. "I guess we will just play it by ear."

They stood just inside the door, letting their eyes adjust to the dim lighting, realizing there was a storage room off to the right. They could hear people in the kitchen, the bang of pots and pans unmistakable as they prepared food for the guests ordering from The Met Dining Room. Victoria peered cautiously into the small room, Chelsea close behind her.

They found her sitting on top of a stack of boxes. "Well hello darling sister, look who finally decided to show up!" She jumped down as she said it, both of them registering the gun in her hand.

Chelsea stood beside Victoria and demanded, "Where is Alex? What have you done with him?" It was easy to see he wasn't with her.

"Oh we will get to him. But first, what the hell took you so long?" Rory said, turning from Chelsea back to Victoria.

Victoria stood her ground before answering. "In case you've forgotten I'm supposed to be giving a funeral. Mother dearest showed up, but had decided it was high time I knew the story of how we ended up here. Your cryptic note wasn't her first priority."

Rory snorted. "Today's bedtime story, titled the princess and the pauper. We both know which part I got to play! I was always an afterthought for her!"

Victoria put her hands on her hips. "How many times can I tell you I'm sorry? And why are we bringing Alex into this? He has nothing to do with any of this!"

Rory's smile was wicked as she looked from Victoria to Chelsea. "Because I want you both to suffer and Alex seems to be your common denominator. The best part is, whoever opens the car door to rescue him, will actually be the one to kill him. The car is wired like the fourth of July, just waiting for some hero to come along and save him. And lucky for you two, you have front row seats! Let's go!"

She waved the gun around to usher them out, but Victoria stood her ground. "This isn't what I'm paying you for! I will not agree to watch any such thing!" she said heatedly.

Chelsea frowned, a thought occurring to her that turned her blood to ice. Slowly she started to move away from Victoria.

"Well in case you haven't noticed sister, you're not in charge here! I run this bitch showcase and we're playing by my rules and I say what goes!" Rory's words were biting, but she kept her voice down, knowing there were people close by. They both jumped as a door slamming shut caught their attention.

Chelsea was down the hallway, out the door before they even noticed. As she scanned the street, she quickly spotted the car used for Hudson & Butler. She watched and waited for traffic to pass so she could cross the street. She suddenly realized Kenny, their driver, was opening the back passenger door. She screamed "NO!" before she fell to her knees.

FORTY-EIGHT

Covering her head instinctively, the small explosion at the car brought her to her knees in a wave of fear. She was afraid to look across the street, but more afraid not to know. She was relieved to see Kenny and Alex both getting to their feet. She could see Alex looking her way, trying to cross the street to her. She realized Victoria and Rory had just come out, Rory having a small explosion of her own.

"What the hell? You pay a guy all that money just to get a little shitty explosion like that?" She waved her gun in Victoria's face before announcing. "I guess I will have to be the one to do the dirty work!" Rory said with a disgusted sneer.

Both women watched as the two men tried to cross the street, so focused on them that Rory never noticed Chelsea charging her until it was too late. They went down with a thud, Rory on the bottom, but fighting like hell to get out from under Chelsea. Savagely Chelsea grabbed her ponytail and yanked Rory's head back. "Still not today bitch!"

"Let her go Chelsea or so help me!" She looked up to find Victoria holding the gun on her. "I said let her. . ." Suddenly Victoria went flying as Alex tackled her to the ground.

Feeling Rory start to squirm, Chelsea pulled her ponytail even harder as Rory screamed. "I'm going to kill you bitch!"

She realized with relief police cars were pulling up, officers swarming everywhere, guns drawn. Chelsea jumped off of Rory, her hands in the air as Rory came up swinging. Oblivious to the officers Rory lunged for Chelsea, putting her hands around her throat. Quickly officers came to her rescue, pulling Rory off of her. Chelsea leaned forward clutching her throat and gasping for air as Alex moved to her side. Slowly Chelsea stood up, letting him pull her into him.

They had quite a story to share with more than one officer, but eventually the crowd dispersed and the police cars pulled away. The officer in charge seemed satisfied with their individual stories, but asked them to come down to the station later to make their formal statements.

Paramedics had checked out the two men, no worse for wear than a few scratches and bruises from hitting the pavement. Kenny had been sent home after his minor wounds had been treated by the paramedics, Alex adding a well deserved week of paid vacation to his calendar.

A new town car had been sent to pick up Alex and Chelsea and they both climbed into the back seat with relief. They sat close, but were quiet, still processing what had gone down.

Chelsea broke the silence first. "I can't believe Victoria was in cahoots with Rory. She actually pointed that gun at me! Was she seriously going to protect her sister? I feel like a fool believing anything that ever came out of her mouth!"

Alex nodded. "I know. I was going to warn you when you got to the church, but as you know I never made it there."

Chelsea turned to him sharply. "How did she get you in the car?"

"She drugged Kenny and put on his jacket and hat so I just assumed it was him when I got in the car. I realized too late when she released sleeping gas, but she locked the doors and I couldn't get out. I woke up where you found me."

"She knows all the tricks. How did you know that Rory and Victoria were actually in cahoots together?" she asked.

"After she came to Victoria's house, I hired a bounty hunter to find Rory. Yesterday he took pictures of Rory and Victoria together, but he couldn't get her nailed down to bring her in. In one picture Victoria's handing her what looks like an envelope of cash. A payoff or guilt money, we're not sure." He was wary of her reaction.

Her laugh was bitter. "Oh I think we do. I think Victoria was going to pay her off to kill me. Getting you there was never part of Victoria's plan though. I couldn't believe she pointed that gun at me. If you hadn't been there to tackle her. . ." she let her voice trail off, Alex pulling her closer and kissing the top of her head, wishing he could do more to comfort her.

"I feel like the universe is trying to tell me I should be dead. How many times can one person have a gun pointed at them?" she asked wearily. "Kharma really is a bitch." she added.

"The universe is telling you to be grateful to be alive. You survived a major gunshot wound last year and lived to tell about it. The universe is telling you I'm here for you, I'll catch you every time you fall. I love you Chelsea." Alex squeezed her hard.

She thought about what he said before she turned to look him in the eyes. "I love you too. I thought you were a goner when that car bomb went off. I guess we're both lucky to be alive."

He smiled at her, his eyes shining bright. "I guess we are."

It had been an exhausting day, but as they lay in bed together, Chelsea felt lucky to be the one in Alex's arms tonight. It had been their misfortune that Victoria had been released at the same time they had finished giving their statements. As they all came out of the police station together, Victoria had nothing to say, but gave Chelsea a look of pure hatred. Alex turned Chelsea towards their car, his arm tight around her.

On their way home she worried what it would take to end this toxic love triangle the three of them had going on. She assumed Alex worried about the same thing. With a variety of charges against Rory, she would be locked up for a long time, but Victoria was a different story. Victoria had the means to avoid being prosecuted for the hit and run manslaughter charge for her father's death. Chelsea wondered if that was the real reason behind not publishing her book. Her hate for him was evidenced throughout the book and could easily be construed as her motive. The preliminary hearing was set for next week and they would all just have to wait and see.

FORTY-NINE

It had been a few days since the latest fiasco in Chelsea's world and once again she poured herself into work to keep herself busy. She sat at her desk surrounded by short piles of manuscripts, each needing her attention as she was the final decision for a rejection or a congratulations letter. She found one much harder to send than the other, knowing every author poured their heart and soul into their manuscript. Suddenly there was a sharp knock on the door and she looked up expectantly.

She was startled to see that it was Victoria. "What the hell are you doing here?" She asked with a mix of nervous incredulousness.

"We need to talk." Victoria said calmly as she removed her oversized hat and sunglasses.

"How did you get past security? Alex gave strict orders he's to be notified if you enter the building."

"I believe I told you once, I trump Alex at Hudson & Butler any day of the week." she said smugly as she sat in the chair across from Chelsea.

"I have nothing to say to you Victoria. Please go!" Chelsea spat out the words.

"Fine. I just need you to listen. I want you to give a statement to the police that I was with you in my office when my father was run down. You remember coming to see me that day, correct?" Victoria stared at her, her look daring her to deny it.

"I was already asked to give my statement regarding that day. They know what time I arrived at your home and it's in our car service logs. They would know I was lying." Chelsea said doubtfully.

"You're creative. You can make something up. And the car log can be taken care of, leave that to me." Victoria said persuasively.

"You can't be serious? After all the shit you've put me through, you think I would risk perjury to help you?"

"Actually I'm very serious. I won't go to prison for the death of my father."

For the first time, Chelsea wondered if Victoria had actually been the one to run him down. She had always assumed it was Rory posing as her, another attempt to ruin her life. "Did you kill your father Victoria?" she asked curiously.

"That's not the point! I will not risk a trial and I need your statement for evidence." Chelsea noticed she was starting to look a little rattled.

"If you're innocent Victoria you have nothing to worry about. Wouldn't it be easier to find evidence that Rory framed you? There are plenty of other things she's done to make your life miserable. Why would my statement be so important?"

"You don't need to worry about the why. But, if you do this for me, I will sell my shares to Alex at the price he asked for, which is quite generous of me." Seeing Chelsea's face, she added with a smirk, "You don't know he's trying to buy me out, do you? Tsk, tsk, I guess your relationship really is hanging by a thread."

Regardless that this was news to Chelsea, she was done negotiating farfetched offers from Victoria. She stood up and pointed to her door. "Get out Victoria! I'm not changing my statement and I don't ever want to see you again in my office! Get out! NOW!"

Just at that moment Alex opened the door. He blanched to see Victoria sitting across from Chelsea. "What are you doing here?"

Victoria stood up, looking like the cat that swallowed the canary. "Apparently I'm enlightening your girlfriend about your offer to buy my shares of Hudson & Butler. I've made her an offer I think is quite generous. I'll let her explain it to you as I was just leaving."

Halfway to the door she turned back to Chelsea. "I'll expect to hear from you soon. The decision is yours. For now." And she was gone.

Chelsea took a deep breath and sat down, realizing she was shaking. "I never want to see that bitch again!"

Alex stood by her desk, uncertain what he could say to make it better. "I didn't want to tell you and get your hopes up until it was a done deal and she had agreed to sell me her shares."

She looked up at him before going to stand to look out her window. He waited for her to collect her thoughts before finally asking, "Are you going to tell me what she wanted?"

"She wants me to change my statement that I was already at her home when her father was hit by a car. If I do that for her, she will sell you Hudson & Butler for what you asked." She glanced at him briefly, hearing him swear under his breath.

"I need to get out of town for a while, Alex. I can't stay here knowing she can just pop up like that anytime it suits her." Chelsea's voice was quiet but the pressure of it all was evident.

Alex came to stand behind her, wrapping his arms around her waist, his chin on her shoulder. "I'm happy to hear you say that because I've been thinking about going to Chicago for a long weekend and would love for you to come with me. It's way past time for you to meet my family. Would you come with me?"

She didn't look at him, but just nodded. "Yes. Yes I'll come with you. I can be packed by tonight."

Alex hugged her and said, "I'll make arrangements." As she continued to stare out the window, he recognized she was at her breaking point. Time away would be good, even if it meant meeting his family.

FIFTY

It had been a few days since Victoria had popped into Chelsea's office uninvited. Alex had been desperate to get Victoria in check and had finally come up with a plan of his own. Now he sat in the car, his entire body humming as they crossed over the bridge into Brooklyn. He had rehearsed what he was going to say to Victoria a hundred times over, but knowing she was unpredictable made him slightly nervous. He checked his watch before giving Chelsea a call. He wanted to make sure she was home and to let her know he would be home within the hour, having some business to take care of first. He offered to take her out to dinner, but she suggested they get take out instead.

Mentally he cussed Victoria, blaming her for Chelsea's current state of mind. The restraining order had been helpful, but if this meeting went the way he planned, she would be feeling much better in no time. As the car pulled into the familiar circle drive, he braced himself for what was sure to come. The housekeeper let him in, but he waved her off, not wanting her to announce him before he let himself into Victoria's office. When he knocked lightly on the door, she looked up expectantly from her desk, her surprise to see him evident.

She stood up as she greeted him. "Alex, this is a nice surprise!"

"It won't be for long I'm afraid." he announced grimly as he sat his briefcase on her desk to open it and retrieve a file.

She kept her expression friendly, "What fun and games did you bring all the way out here? Has Chelsea decided to change her statement after all?"

"I'm here to sever ties with you Victoria. I told you once to figure out how to make it work with Chelsea and you've done nothing but cause her grief. I won't keep putting her or myself in this position." His voice was tight but firm.

Victoria's eyes were glittering with rage as she responded to him. "Always Prince Charming ready and able to catch the office slut when she falls. How quaint." Her voice dripped with sarcasm.

He ignored her attempt to bait him and handed her the file instead. He watched as she came to realize it was a contract to buy out her shares of Hudson & Butler. She tossed it back to him with "That's a hard pass Alex."

Alex sat down in the chair across from her and crossed his ankle over his knee, his hands behind his head. "You seem to think you have a choice. Perhaps you want to read through the contract a little closer." His casual confidence both irked her and made her question just what was happening here.

"I don't think a hostile takeover is applicable in this situation. Again, I pass, no thank you." She refused to pick it up, her expression daring him to press the matter any further.

His hands stayed on his head, his eyes taking on their own glint. "Remember how you wrote our original contract to give yourself the majority of shares to protect yourself? Well you were so arrogant, so self-absorbed that you didn't pay any attention to the amendment I added to protect myself. I asked you to read it, but you signed it anyway. You might want to peruse it now."

He watched as she started to falter, her voice icy. "Why would I need to read it? We were engaged and I trusted you!"

"Oh I know. You made a point to show me how much you trusted me when you created a forty/sixty partnership. It's time to let Hudson

& Butler start a new chapter without you. You will see my offer is quite generous. I have a pen if you need one." His eyes were steely, trying to leave her no room to argue.

"Why would I sell to you Alex? Because you what?" She tossed the contract back at him again, her contempt growing.

"Because you signed a document that if you. . .well actually you should read it for yourself." Alex opened the contract, pointing out the highlighted passage he wanted her to read. He watched her face change from defiance to disbelief to denial.

"My case won't make it to trial Alex. You're wishful thinking isn't going to change anything." She responded.

"It doesn't matter what happens with your case now. You dug yourself a grave when you conspired with a wanted criminal. You pointed a gun at someone willing to testify against you." He still sat back, waiting for her denial.

"When did I conspire with a wanted criminal? What are you talking about?" She bravely tried to sound incredulous.

Finally his hands came down as he pulled some photos from his jacket pocket. "Maybe this will jog your memory." He threw them down on the desk in front of her.

"Where the hell did you get these?" She tried to sound offended, but he could see the shock to see he had pictures of her handing an envelope to Rory.

"Checkmate Victoria. I'm here to present this contract in person out of respect to the relationship we've had in the past. But if I leave here without your signature, I have an email drafted and waiting for me to hit send to our board of directors. I also have a press conference scheduled for nine o'clock tomorrow morning to make a major announcement regarding Hudson & Butler. Like I said, I have a pen if you need it." He kept his voice cool and collected.

As her eyes started to fill with tears, he put his hand up to stop her. "Spare me the waterworks. The only thing I need from you is your signature." He said, holding out a pen to her.

She snatched it from him, angrily scribbling her name in the spots highlighted with little sticky yellow arrows. "Just don't put her name on the door!" she demanded.

"In the morning I will announce our new name is Butler Publishing and introduce Chelsea as my new CEO. I've arranged for a reporter with the New York Times to do a full page interview with her. But her name won't be on the door. Yet."

Alex took the signed document from Victoria and put it back in his briefcase. He kept his expression neutral as he walked to the door.

He turned back to her to share one more thing. "By the way, I took Chelsea to apply for a restraining order against you. A judge approved her request as of ten this morning. I know you have money for the fine, but I also know you don't want to do the time if you violate the order. Stay the hell away from her. If you even think you smell Chelsea's perfume, let alone see her, you better be turning and running the other way. Take care Victoria." With that he was gone, ignoring her look of rage.

He climbed into the car and sat back, taking a deep breath before releasing it. It was over. This chapter was finally closed, but a new one was just beginning. He closed his eyes and thought of Chelsea. He couldn't wait to tell her it was a done deal. He had made a choice and had no regrets. He loved Chelsea and he couldn't wait to spend the rest of his life with her. He looked forward to their visit to Chicago, but first he had a phone call to make. He would rather say it in person, but given the circumstances, a phone call should work just fine.

FIFTY-ONE

She sat looking out the window, aimlessly watching the landscape pass under their plane, fluffy white clouds leaving small shadows below sporadically. Alex sat next to her reading the paper, his arm warm beside her as it rested on the bar between them. She couldn't stop thinking about the past twenty-four hours, a whirlwind, but for once in a good way. Mostly.

Chelsea had jumped for joy when Alex told her the news that he owned Hudson & Butler outright, now simply known as Butler Publishing. He had insisted they go out to dinner and celebrate giving her a quick thirty minutes to pull her look together. They had reservations at Balthazar, an iconic French brasserie in the heart of SoHo. Their steak frites, one of Chelsea's favorites, were all the motivation she needed to quickly shower and put on one of her favorite little black dresses.

They had been seated quickly, the red banquette cozy as they perused their menus. Chelsea usually feasted on their steak frites, but tonight's special was Coq Au Vin, one of her favorites in any upscale eatery. They shared a bottle of champagne, their flutes filled with bubbles as they toasted Alex's big news.

"Congrats on becoming the sole proprietor of the hottest new publishing sensation, Butler Publishing! I'm so proud of you and happy to be on this journey with you! Cheers to you Alex!" She said, her voice full of happiness for both of them.

They had finished eating when Alex had nervously announced he had something to ask her and he wanted her to think about it before she responded. Her heart had skipped a beat as she couldn't help but wonder if he was going to propose. Suddenly she wished she had worn the other little black dress.

Her acute disappointment had been short lived as his question caught her off guard. She could still see his proud smile, his eyes warm as he asked her to be his CEO. She had taken a sip of champagne before declining his offer. She could see the disappointment in his face before he quickly masked it, picking up his own flute for a sip.

She had hurried to explain herself. She had told him being a CEO was the highest form of a compliment he could give her, but she didn't want to run his company for him. She loved her job of nurturing authors to find the best version of their stories. She reminded him no one was better qualified to be CEO than he was. He had been doing it for years, but now he had the freedom to make changes to bring his company into the twenty-first century. She had assured him she would be right beside him, supporting him anywhere he needed her to.

He had agreed with her, knowing what she said was true. He smiled at her as he said, "As I recall, that's how you got hired in the first place. It's good to know you have my back."

After dinner they had laid together happily, Alex telling her, "We're free of her. It's time to start our own chapter."

She had kissed him lightly before turning her back to him, always loving when he would pull her into him tightly, his arms around her protectively. Long after he was asleep, she had laid awake, her mind reeling with a variety of thoughts. She thought about how Alex had played CEO for Victoria and how in the end it had not worked out so well for them, one's power put into play ruining their relationship.

She thought about how excited she had been thinking for a split second that Alex was going to propose to her. She couldn't deny her disappointment when he hadn't pulled out a ring after all. She had set her sights on Alex over a year ago, but just recently began to think about his ring on her finger. After almost a year together, she was mostly grateful for the relationship they shared and hopeful a ring would be part of their new chapter together.

She had smiled when he made reference to how she got her job with Hudson & Butler, but actually wondered if Alex was reminding them both of her place in the company, the office slut as Victoria had referred to her weeks ago. Maybe she wasn't the type of girl a man like Alex would marry. In the morning she would pack conservatively for Chicago, wanting nothing more than to make a good impression on Alex's family.

Earlier this morning she had been proud to stand beside Alex during his press conference and then later do her interview with the reporter from the New York Times. She had chosen to wear a creme silk tank with a pair of high waisted black pants. She had completed her look with her lucky gold Coco Chanel belt. There had also been a photographer, taking several pictures of her outside their building on the streets of Manhattan as well as in her office. She had tried to answer the questions eloquently, hoping to make both herself and Butler Publishing look good.

Now as Alex folded the paper, she turned to look at him. "Well? How did I do? Did he make me look good?" She realized she was nervous to hear what he had to say about her interview and the article in the New York Times.

"You were amazing. The pictures of you are stunning. Your answers to his questions were perfect. You articulated how smart you are, but something even more important than that." Alex was beaming at her and Chelsea couldn't help but return his smile.

"What's more important than that?" she asked curiously.

Unexpectedly he put his hand to her chest. "You showed him your heart. How much you care about our authors, how much time and energy you put into each of them to bring their stories to life." He picked up her hand and kissed it. "Well done Chelsea. You will have a plethora of authors wanting to work with you at Butler Publishing. I'm so proud of you!"

Chelsea was floored. She had never thought of herself as someone with heart. That was for people who were weak and easily manipulated by bitches like herself.

"That's not all. He reached out to Kat about you." Kat had been her first customer and the initial reason she had come to Hudson & Butler more than a year ago. Alex folded the paper back and found Kat's quote before handing it to her. "Here, read it for yourself."

> *"Chelsea Logan is the real deal when you're looking for an editor. It was my privilege to be her first client and together we've grown to be at the top of our game through Butler Publishing. I'm forever grateful for all of her creative expertise in nurturing my books to be the best they can be and making me a New York Times Bestselling author."*

Chelsea didn't know what to think. She remembered back to their first encounter and what a bitch she had been to Kat. She was startled to realize how times could change, admitting to herself no one had ever said something so nice about her. Watching her face, Alex laughed softly and pulled her in for a hug.

"Authors are going to love you Chelsea Logan. Just like I do. It's your time to shine." He kissed her on her mouth, keeping it light.

"I should text Kat and thank her." she said.

"You can thank her tonight. We have dinner reservations with them at RPM, a new Italian place you are going to love!"

She turned back to her window, the sunny blue skies calming her. Everything was moving pretty fast right now, all seemingly in a good direction. She couldn't help but let a smile come to her lips, unable to deny the happiness she was feeling. Maybe it finally was her time to shine, maybe Alex was onto something.

FIFTY-TWO

The two couples sat at a discreet table in the upscale trendy restaurant, deep into their truffled garlic bread, glasses of wine all around. They were making light conversation as they waited for their food to be prepared. Chelsea was looking forward to Mama DePandi's Pomodoro as well as trying a bite of Alex's gorgonzola wagyu steak. She was a foodie through and through, enjoying nothing better than to share good food with people she loved. As she sipped her wine, she smiled to herself, knowing she was lucky to be sitting there with her three most favorite people in the world.

She realized Alex was talking about the article in the paper, giving Kat props for getting the new name of his publishing company in her comment. He turned to Chelsea expectantly.

Putting her glass down, she chimed in too. "Yes, thank you Kat for your kind words. I really appreciate you saying that about me too. Your checks in the mail!" She laughed teasingly.

Alex smiled. "You'll have to forgive her. She struggles with taking compliments."

Chelsea looked at them both, defensive. "No, no, I was kidding about your check. It just surprised me to see your words in print."

Kat paused, thinking about it. "I get that. We didn't start off on the best of terms, you being the absurd bitch that you were and me the naive small town girl I was. But regardless of your personal bullshit, you did work hard to make my book the best seller that it is. You've found your niche and you're good at it. Just read the paper, he'll tell you all about it, if you don't believe me!" Kat said with a laugh.

Anxious to move on, Chelsea looked from Kat to Thomas, her face turning serious. "Do you all realize what today is?"

Immediately the table became somber, Alex putting his hand on her leg under the tablecloth. She suddenly realized that's why they were all sitting there together tonight having dinner. Of course she should have known Alex would remember.

It was Thomas who spoke first. "It's the one year anniversary of you saving my life."

Chelsea's face was a mix of shame and regret. "I only had to save your life because I put it in danger to begin with! And because, you know, I care about you." She turned to Kat and added, "And I care about you too Kat! It's surreal to me that we're sitting here having dinner as friends!"

Kat was the one to break the tension. "Friends *and* the best of the best in publishing, thank *you* very much!" she said with a smile.

Alex raised his glass, the other three quickly following his lead. "Cheers to success, good friends, and love." As they clinked their glasses together, her eyes met Thomas's.

She took a sip of her wine before adding to his toast. "I will never be able to say this enough, but I'm so sorry for all the bullshit I put you both through, especially you Thomas. Thank you for your forgiveness and for giving me a second chance. You all mean the world to me."

They were all silently sipping their wine when dinner arrived. The small talk subsided temporarily as they dug in, happily enjoying their food. Chelsea was nothing but grateful as she remembered back to a year ago. In a way, getting shot had saved her life as much as it had jeopardized it. She was a different person now. She had purpose in her work and enjoyed her role as an editor, just recently promoted to senior editor, her terms negotiated under the sheets with Alex. They both knew she was worth every penny for what she got done in the office and assumed anyone worth their salt in the office knew it too.

Tomorrow she would meet Alex's family and she could only hope it would go well knowing how important his family was to him. She would be on her best behavior knowing there would be no bullshitting his mother. Tonight though, they were staying in a hotel not far from RPM, Alex wanting to show her his own version of his hometown before they caught up with his family tomorrow afternoon. As she finished her glass of wine, she pushed tomorrow aside, happy to be alive and enjoying tonight. Who knew what the weekend would bring.

FIFTY-THREE

Her large suitcase lay on the bed, her clothes in disarray as she attempted to reorganize it. Through the open window she could hear Alex and his mother talking quietly in the backyard. The string of outdoor lights shone up into their bedroom and she could hear the fire pit crackle and pop from time to time. The house was quiet, everyone long since gone home, although Alex's twin nieces had begged to spend the night with GiGi. Chelsea had peeked in on them before coming to Alex's bedroom to start packing and give him and his mother some time alone.

The weekend had been a whirlwind of loud voices, laughter, occasional squabbles among the littles, and gentle ribbing among the siblings. His mother was at the center of it all, keeping the chaos organized and enjoyable. Chelsea had never been around anything like Alex's family, but she had been a chameleon her whole life and was quick to adapt as needed. She started out as an observer, but eventually his twin nieces had pulled her into their friendly game of badminton. Chelsea had been playing tennis ever since she could remember, and the twins had been impressed she could handle a racquet so well.

She caught Alex watching her, his expression amused to see her take the game so seriously. They had played tennis together occasionally and he knew first hand how competitive she could be. It turned out the losers had to clean up dirty dishes after dining outside on grilled chicken, fresh fruit and pasta salad. It was Chelsea's turn to watch in amusement as Alex became the head dishwasher, handing out wet dishes to be dried.

After s'mores had been made and devoured, the littles had gotten into pajamas and were sprawled out in the family room watching a movie. Chelsea soon discovered this was how the adults got time to themselves to have their own conversations. She listened as they talked about everything from the Cubs finishing a decent season to the current presidential race as President Obama worked to secure a second term.

They had regrouped Saturday morning for bagels and donuts before heading out to explore the Field Museum. After that they headed to Giordano's to have the world famous pizza for a late lunch. When the littles started asking to go and ride the ferris wheel, the adults protested until one of the twins loudly suggested 'Aunt Chelsea' should be the one to decide since she was the guest after all.

With all eyes on her, Chelsea had bravely responded. "I say we get Uncle Alex and we do it!" She couldn't help but smile when they cheered for her.

As they went to grab a taxi, Alex leaned over and asked, "Who are you?"

Chelsea had merely shrugged and replied lightly, "When in Chicago, do what the littles want."

He laughed and nodded agreement. "You always were a fast learner. And it is good to be loved!"

Finally getting her suitcase put back together, Chelsea had a smile on her face as she thought about the weekend shenanigans. She had her clothes laid out and ready for their early flight home to New York in the morning. There was a light knock on the door before Alex entered.

She turned to him announcing "I just finished packing!"

He went to her and kissed her before pulling her close. "It's my turn now. Why don't you go and enjoy the end of the fire with my mom."

Chelsea was about to decline politely when she realized it wasn't really a question. "Of course." she answered, faking her smile. She knew she was in with the littles, but she had no idea where she stood with the family matriarch.

As she came to join her, Alex's mother handed her a light fleece blanket. "You may want to wrap this around you if you get cold. The fire is warm, but only to a certain extent."

Realizing this was the first time they had been alone together, she nervously hoped she wasn't speaking metaphorically.

"Thank you." Chelsea said, accepting it graciously.

"Would you like a glass of wine? We have a pinot noir open at the moment." his mother asked.

Chelsea shook her head. "I had one at dinner. I'm good, thank you."

She cocked her head and asked, "You don't drink much do you?"

"Neither Alex nor I do. I guess because our workouts are first thing in the mornings." Chelsea answered, her voice quiet.

She was surprised when Alex's mother gave a short laugh. "I have noticed Alex is drinking less. I guess we have you to thank for that!" Seeing her confusion, his mother continued. "Alex loved to party as a teenager. Then he met his first wife, Victoria in college and she was always dragging him to all kinds of social events and shoving a drink in his hand. According to Alex."

Sensing Chelsea stiffen at the mention of Victoria's name, Alex's mother changed subject. "What were you like as a teenager?"

Chelsea hesitated, then remembered she would see right through her. "I was hell on wheels. My mother was an alcoholic and my father worked all the time. I did what I wanted." She shrugged, not sure what else to say.

His mother's look was kind as she said, "And look at you now. So successful, doing something you love. Alex tells me you're quite good. He's lucky to have you."

Chelsea smiled. She could imagine him saying that. "He can't help himself. He has to say that."

With one eyebrow raised, his mother asked, "Why? Because he loves you?"

Chelsea was startled to hear her say that, but answered with, "No, because he hired me!"

They both laughed, Chelsea relieved to be finding some common ground in talking about Alex. Just as quickly, his mother became serious again. "But he does love you. We can all see it in his face. You make him happy, happier than he's been in a long time."

Chelsea was shocked to hear this, always assuming she was the one lucky to be getting the good end of their relationship. To hear her words meant a lot to her. "I love him too, Mrs. Butler. I want nothing more than to make him happy. I'm not sure I deserve someone like Alex."

"Why do you say that? If you love him and make him happy, what more can one ask for?" she asked.

Chelsea stared into the flames of the fire, choosing her words carefully. "My family's not like yours. There's so much love here. I see why Alex is the generous loving man he is. I've made some pretty awful mistakes in my past."

She snorted before announcing, "Nonsense! That's how people grow, through their mistakes. You think Alex hasn't made any mistakes? I believe you've met Victoria. He's made his fair share, but he always had his family to come back to and remind him of who he was raised to be. From what Alex tells me, you've been taking care of yourself for a long time and you deserve someone to take care of you too. When you love someone, taking care of them comes naturally."

Chelsea thought about what she was saying. She would like to think her crap choices were limited to her younger years, when in fact they had followed her into her thirties, not that long ago. Not wanting to elaborate, she said, "Thank you Mrs Butler." and left it at that.

"I want you to remember something for me. True love is endless. It doesn't matter who you are, who your family is, how much money you have or don't have. True love is given unconditionally. I know my son loves you. Embrace it Chelsea and let yourself be happy. You've made it, there's nothing left to prove to yourself or anyone. Does that make sense?"

Chelsea nodded, a lump in her throat preventing her from speaking. She had always thought money was the answer to happiness, but she realized now happiness was an inside job, something you gave yourself and others. She stood as his mother stood too. She watched as she threw some water on the fire before taking Chelsea's arm and walking into the house with her. "One more thing. Please call me Martha."

Chelsea smiled at her. "Good night Martha. And thank you for all your kind words."

Martha pulled her in to give her a hug. "Good night dear. I'll see you bright and early before you fly back to New York. You and Alex will be back here for the holidays before you know it. You think this was loud? Wait until you see my four grandbabies around a Christmas tree! It's pure joy. For all of us." Her eyes were bright as she stopped in front of Alex's door, whispering "sweet dreams."

Alex was sitting up in bed reading as he waited for her. "Well? How was your talk?" he asked with a smile.

Chelsea army crawled her way to him across the bed. "It was good, but I'm exhausted!" she said as she curled up under his arm. "I think she likes me though." she added.

He laughed. "I know she does! And why wouldn't she?"

Chelsea yawned letting Alex pull the covers up over her. She was asleep in no time, still wrapped in his arms. Her sleep was deep, her dreams sweet just like Martha had wished for her when they said goodnight. She dreamed that Alex was asking her to marry him, professing how much he loved her. He was down on one knee, holding out the most beautiful ring she had ever seen, the Eiffel tower sparkling almost as brightly in the night behind him.

She woke up with a start automatically reaching for Alex. He was snoring softly beside her, one arm still across her. She relaxed back into her pillows. She lay beside him wondering why the Eiffel Tower had been part of her dream. Her life had been a whirlwind of the good and the bad the last couple of weeks, but clearly her subconscious was still holding onto Paris. She closed her eyes, wanting to go back to her sweet dream with Alex. After all she hadn't had a chance to say yes to his proposal. Yet.

EPILOGUE

She ran along the street, her daily route familiar to her by now. The Rue Saint-Dominique was the best known street from which to take pictures of the iconic Eiffel Tower, but for Chelsea it was a gorgeous way to start the day, her early morning run timed with the sunrise and the promise of a new day.

She always took a break in front of the Eiffel Tower, giving herself a moment to take it all in and feel grateful for where she was. She drank her water, enjoying the peace and quiet of the early morning hours, knowing it would soon be bustling with Parisians and tourists alike within a matter of hours. She had been in Paris for a couple of weeks now and relished in her new routines. Today she was particularly reflective, knowing that Alex would be arriving tomorrow.

It had been his idea for her to stick to hosting Butler Publishing's first ever writer's retreat. Chelsea had put out feelers weeks before and Alex had decided it was a move in a new direction he wanted to take with his company. The world was a big place and there was no reason not to reach across the big pond to European authors as well.

It was hard to believe it had been only three weeks ago that he had surprised her, coming into her office and handing her an itinerary along with a boarding pass to Paris. He had finalized arrangements and had a pile of twenty-five applicant's for the retreat. Set up in two stages, the first weekend of the retreat would be for a large group of writers attending workshops and working in small groups based on their greatest writing needs. From the weekend's events, five authors would be invited to stay for the next two weeks to work closely with Chelsea, her editorial genius at their disposal as they worked to establish their stories in one of the most iconic cities in the world.

It turned out that Victoria's case was going to trial and Chelsea had been grateful to have her ticket to Paris ready and waiting. She worried about Alex going through it without her there and had made him promise to join her the last week she was here. How could she truly enjoy the city of love without him? He had agreed and now that day was almost upon them.

She closed up her water bottle and took one more appreciative look around as she headed back to her hotel ready to finish her run for the day. Thinking of her warm croissant with jam and a large coffee was all the motivation she needed. She didn't even realize a man in running clothes stood discreetly watching her.

He had turned away from her as she glanced in his direction, relief washing over him as she started back to her hotel, her run at a brisk pace. As he followed her, his mind reeled with excitement thinking of what lay ahead for them. He knew her Paris routines well by now, his need to know she was safe not easily dismissed.

He had arrived late last night, heading straight for the hotel, staying on the floor above hers. He was waiting for her when she came out of the hotel, his tired body warmed up and ready for a run. It made him smile to see her, having to resist his urge to run to her and pick her up in a big embrace. It had been a couple of weeks since he had dropped her at JFK airport for the long nonstop flight to Paris.

He wasn't a fan of Facetime, but it had been better than nothing. He could tell she was doing well and he was relieved she had not had to deal with the shenanigans of Victoria's trial. It had gotten messy when he had been subpoenaed as a character witness. But that was all behind him now.

Tonight he would show up unexpectedly at dinner, and later suggest that they walk to the Eiffel Tower where he had every intention of asking her to marry him. He had arranged for champagne to be waiting for them when they got back to their hotel. He was very much looking forward to celebrating their impending nuptials and building their life together minus Victoria. It would be a night to remember and the beginning of a new chapter for them both.